Mr. *and* Mrs. HADDOCK,
in Paris, *France*

Books by
Donald Ogden Stewart

A Parody Outline of History
Perfect Behavior
Aunt Polly's Story of Mankind
Mr. and Mrs. Haddock Abroad
The Crazy Fool
Mr. and Mrs. Haddock in Paris, France

Mr. *and* Mrs. Haddock *in* Paris, *France*

BY

DONALD OGDEN STEWART

With Drawings by

herb roth

HARPER & BROTHERS *Publishers*
New York *and* London MCMXXVI

Mr. *and* Mrs. HADDOCK *in* Paris, *France*

First Edition   H-A

To
Gerald and Sara Murphy

ILLUSTRATIONS

Mr. *and* Mrs. HADDOCK,
in Paris, *France*

Mr. *and* Mrs. Haddock *in* Paris, *France*

CHAPTER I

"OH, but you can't know *Paris*," murmured the nice lady sitting opposite Mr. Haddock in the first-class railroad compartment, "unless you live on the *rive gauche*."

"That mean *'the left bank,'*" immediately volunteered little Mildred—Mr. Haddock's daughter—who spoke French but with an accent.

"The left bank of *what?*" asked Mr. Haddock, wiping the perspiration from his forehead.

"Why—the *Seine*," replied the lady, slightly condescendingly.

"A river in France," patiently explained the "little girl interpreter."

"Don't you suppose I know that?" demanded her father.

"No," replied Mildred promptly, and turning to the lady she announced, with a faint Continental shrug, *"Mon père* is in the lumber business and reads *très peu."*

"Mildred," said Mr. Haddock, reaching for a ball bat or a stout two-inch piece of iron pipe, "do you want papa to be cross?"

There had been, as a matter of fact, a considerable amount of condensed irritation in that railway carriage now speeding across France toward Paris. In the first place, Mrs. Haddock was feeling a little seasick now that the ocean voyage from America was over, and in the second place little Mildred didn't have any handkerchief, and in the third place Mr. Haddock had had an argument just before the train started with a French baggage porter which Mr. Haddock had lost, but which he was going to take to a Higher Court as soon as he could find out from Thomas Cook and Son or the American Express Company how to *get* to a Higher Court.

But anger and irritation were not what Mr. Haddock had come three thousand miles to find, and the country through which they were now passing was very sunny and very peaceful, and as he leaned back against the white crocheted head-rest and gazed out at the passing greenness of what looked a lot like wheat he gradually began to think of forgiving the French baggage porter for not speaking English.

"Well, Hattie," he said, patting his wife on the hand and pointing out of the window to a sign which read "Lucky Strike Cigarettes," "we're in France at last."

Just then the train shrieked its way into a long smoky tunnel.

"It looks a lot like America," was little Mildred's comment after the second minute of darkness, lighted only by a small blue lamp over their heads.

"I'm pretty sure it's France," said her father, "but we can always ask;" and when the compartment finally emerged once more into the sunshine he looked to the lady across from him for confirmation.

"Yes," she nodded, "it's France—*my* France." And she sighed deeply.

[3]

Mr. and Mrs. Haddock

"It's *her* France, Hattie," said Mr. Haddock, a new note of respect in his voice.

Mrs. Haddock, surveying calmly the redness of many poppies amid the fresh verdure of French fields, was reminded (by the sight of a distant cemetery) to look up once more at the rack over Mr. Haddock's head to see if the bags were all there.

The bags *were* all there, but she was not sure she had locked *both* locks on the new suitcase after that silly examination at the Customs. It worried her, as did also the thought that it would have been safer to have packed her son's wife's picture in Mr. Haddock's pajamas. Broken glass was very dangerous, and if Mildred cut herself it would probably be impossible to get any Peroxide of Hydrogen, or Iodine in a place like Paris. Blood poisoning set in very rapidly, and before the doctor could arrive Mildred might lose the arm as far as the elbow. This would also undoubtedly bring on one of Mr. Haddock's heart attacks and she was not sure in which bag she had put Dr. Kendall's pills. She

groaned, and removed a spot of egg or something from Mr. Haddock's left trouser leg.

But the faint distant pealing of a church
bell in a square white stone tower carried her
attention once more to the mellow French
landscape, and her mind unconsciously began
to run in tune to the eternal rhythm of the
Old World.

"Will," she said, "I think you tipped that
smoking room steward too much."

"A capital fellow," replied her husband,
"with a wife and eight children in Baden-
Baden—all girls."

"Fiddlesticks!" said Mrs. Haddock. "And
you were a fool to give that French maid a
cent. She didn't do a thing but make eyes at
that silly bath steward all week."

"Ah," said Mr. Haddock, "the French—a
wonderful little people," and he made as
though to place an imaginary wreath at the
tomb of the unknown soldier.

"You gave her a hundred francs," insisted
Mrs. Haddock.

"If you knew," sighed the lady opposite,

[5]

"what a hundred francs mean to a Frenchman."

"I'm beginning to learn," said Mr. Haddock with an involuntary grimace.

"Ah—" she murmured, "but if you Americans only knew the *real* French people."

"Aren't you an American?" asked Mr. Haddock.

"I live in New York," she replied.

"Oh," said Mr. Haddock. "Excuse us," and in a well meaning effort to atone for his blunder he whistled nervously and remarked "An interesting city—and full of charm for the casual visitor, as well as stimulating to the imagination of poets and writers the world over."

The lady made no answer to this, and as a result there was an awkward pause in the conversation.

Little Mildred, however, broke the ice.

"Are you a Jew?" she asked.

"Am I a Jewess?" asked the lady, and she shook her head. "No."

"You see, Mildred," said Mr. Haddock,

"it's *Jewess*—not Jew. You owe me forty cents," and he explained to the lady that he and his daughter often amused themselves in spare moments by playing a game called "Grammar."

"I should think," remarked the lady, "that the little girl might also play a game called 'Deportment.' "

"Thirty cents," argued Mildred.

"Forty," said her father.

"Thirty," insisted Mildred, and she counted on her fingers. "Four 'ain'ts' is twenty, one 'lay down' makes a quarter—and 'Jew' is thirty."

"How about 'bastard'?" asked her father.

"How about it?" replied the daughter a little belligerently.

"You called that porter a bastard," said her father.

"Did I use the right tense?" asked Mildred.

"Yes," admitted her father.

"And the right mood?"

Mr. Haddock shook his head reminiscently in the affirmative.

[7]

"Well, then, thirty cents," said Mildred, and the argument was closed.

Mildred and her mother got up and went out to look for a glass of water.

"A bright girl," said Mr. Haddock to the lady.

"If you knew," she replied, "if you knew how it affects me to hear a little child talk like that!"

"Ah," said Mr. Haddock, "if I knew so many things! If I knew, for example," he continued—"if I knew who has been in the lavatory for the last twenty minutes!" and he bit off the end of a cigar savagely and made as though to smoke.

"*Non fumeurs,*" said the lady instantly, pointing to a sign over Mr. Haddock's head.

"What's that mean?" asked Mr. Haddock.

" 'Do not smoke,' " replied the lady happily.

"Well, well," said Mr. Haddock, "I seem to be learning the language quite rapidly—'*Occupé*' and '*Non Fumeurs*' and '*Nicht Hinauslehnen*'—and I've only been in France a couple of hours."

[8]

"That last isn't French," objected the lady. "It's German."

"It's written on the window," said Mr. Haddock and he pointed.

"The French is just above it," explained the lady, " *'Il est dangereux de se pencher au dehors!'*—and the third line is Italian."

"Indeed," said Mr. Haddock, and he repeated the phrase several times to himself.

"Who knows," he added, "but that some day my gift for tongues may become quite a factor in promoting International Peace and Good Will." And he threw his cigar out of the window in a manner that would tend to do away with "All War."

Mildred returned with an announcement.

"There isn't any drinking water in the car," she said.

Mrs. Haddock corroborated this.

Mr. Haddock took out a notebook and pencil.

"No water on train," he wrote, and after that he added, *"See about this Tuesday, sure."*

"There," he said, "that takes care of that,"

[9]

and he put the notebook back in his pocket with a happy smile.

"But I'm thirsty," said little Mildred, "and there isn't any water."

"You forget, my dear," said Mr. Haddock, "that France is a *wine*-drinking country. We must try and adapt ourselves as soon as possible to French ways and French customs."

"Well, then," said little Mildred, "I think I shall drink some wine."

"You shall not," said Mrs. Haddock immediately.

"French children drink wine," said little Mildred.

"And eat frogs," added her mother, disapprovingly.

"I ate a frog once," said little Mildred, "and it made me very sick. First there was a terrible retching at my stomach and then ——"

"If you please," objected the lady, "I would rather not hear about it."

"Why not?" asked little Mildred.

"Possibly, my dear," suggested Mr. Haddock, "the lady has a pet frog at home. How

[10]

would you like it if some one ate Alice, your rabbit?"

"I'd love it," said little Mildred. "I don't like that rabbit. All she does is have little rabbits."

"Motherhood," said her father, "is a noble career." And he patted Mrs. Haddock proudly on the knee.

"Oh! Look!" cried little Mildred. "We're coming into a town."

The train slackened speed as it passed from roads to streets and from fields to houses. Old carts with old drivers waiting at crossings, with an occasional foreign-looking automobile and the chauffeur in a white coat; narrow streets; walls; gardens; then more and more white stone houses; and finally the Hôtel de la Gare.

The train imperceptibly came to a rest in the station; the nice lady got up and left.

"Maybe this is Paris," said Mrs. Haddock, worried. "Will, maybe this is Paris!"

Mr. Haddock stuck his head out the window.

"I don't see the Eiffel Tower," he said.

[11]

"Isn't there some sort of a sign on the station?" asked his wife, becoming more and more nervous.

"There are several signs," replied Mr. Haddock, "and either this is the town of *Cabinets Gratuets* or *Chef de Gare* or *Sortie*—it's rather hard to tell which."

" *'Sortie'* means 'exit,' " said little Mildred.

" 'Exit' is a funny name for a town," was Mrs. Haddock's comment.

"Sh-h-h, dear," cautioned Mr. Haddock, putting his finger to his lips. "We must not be too critical. Above everything else we want the French to like us and we don't want them to think that we are always comparing them with ourselves. Perhaps," he continued, observing on the platform outside ten or twelve members of the Legion of Honor excitedly discussing Racine, "it would even help if I grew a beard."

"You will do nothing of the kind," said Mrs. Haddock.

"But, my dear," said her husband, "think what a graceful gesture that would be. Think what it would accomplish in the way of cementing the friendly relations between Lafayette's country and ours!"

At that moment the compartment door was opened and a French lady dressed in black and carrying a small dog peered in.

Mr. Haddock smiled amiably.

The lady turned to her companion, shrugged, remarked, *"Américains,"* closed the door and passed on down the aisle.

"I wonder how she knew," said Mr. Haddock.

As he spoke, the door was once more slid open and another French lady, also dressed in black and carrying a small dog, appeared.

Mr. Haddock stroked his figurative beard reflectively, and with a hasty glance at the window and a slight shrug remarked to his wife:

"Il est dangereux de se pencher au dehors."

"Américains," said the French lady and the door was once more slammed shut.

Mr. Haddock winced and looked at his watch.

"Lafayette is late," he said; and then he

added, "This will make us kinder to the Rosenbergs when we get home, dear."

Mrs. Haddock drew herself up proudly, and the three Americans sat in silence. Suddenly a wisp of smoke drifted in through the window, and Mr. Haddock turned pale.

"My God!" he cried. "They've set fire to the train, and the first American who puts a foot outside will be shot like a dog."

The three looked at one another in dismay.

"Oh dear," said Mrs. Haddock, "I wish we'd gone to London first."

Just then down the aisle came the sound of footsteps.

"Saved!" cried Mr. Haddock. "It's the troops from Fort Dodge."

But it wasn't the troops from Fort Dodge.

It was two people. The man was dressed in a loose tweed suit and the woman was dressed in an old raincoat. They pushed open the door of the compartment and came in, followed by three large pieces of baggage.

The man removed the pipe from his mustache and said something to the woman. The

[14]

language sounded vaguely familiar to Mr. Haddock, and he listened intently for several minutes.

"Either my French is getting better," he said at last, "or else ——" and then he suddenly realized that the lady and the gentleman were talking English.

"Wall, I swan," said Mr. Haddock, spitting on the floor several times, "ef it ain't Hands across the sea—and Mrs. Hands. Shake, pard," and taking some plug tobacco from his pocket, he offered it to his British cousins.

His British cousins paid not the slightest attention. The gentleman, however, coolly began taking Mr. Haddock's baggage down from the rack in order that he might put his own in its place.

"Oh dear!" said Mrs. Haddock, looking at the Haddock luggage lying on the floor and out in the corridor.

Just then a conductor came along and began talking very fast in French.

"I say, what's the beggar want?" asked the Englishman of his wife.

"He says we're on the wrong train—he says this train goes to Paris," she replied.

"Look here, old man," said the Englishman, addressing the conductor, "this train does *not* go to Paris," and he finished with his baggage, sat down, and began to read *The Daily Mail*.

The conductor shrugged his shoulders and disappeared.

"Papa," whispered little Mildred.

"What, dear?" asked her father.

"Papa, may I kick him just once? Please, I won't ask you again."

Mr. Haddock leaned out the window, looked eagerly around, and then shook his head.

"No, dear," he replied. "We have to wait until there is a light in the old North Church," and he silently and thoughtfully busied himself with putting his baggage back wherever he could find room for it.

The engine whistled shrilly. The guards

outside yelled something. Some one else blew another whistle. Then slowly and quietly the train started.

A man came along the corridor ringing a small bell.

"I bet that's for lunch," cried little Mildred, whose instinct in such matters was unfailing.

"I wonder," said Mr. Haddock, "if Americans are allowed to eat with the white folks."

They got up and followed the man down the aisle, and after squeezing their way with difficulty past people standing in the corridors of several coaches, they came at last to the dining car.

They were ushered to a table by the French equivalent of a very polite dining car conductor.

Mrs. Haddock gazed in dismay at three large, empty blue plates piled in front of her.

"I've lost my appetite, Will," she whispered to her husband. "It's all so different."

"Nonsense!" replied Mr. Haddock. "The thing to do is to do what everybody else does."

[17]

Mr. and Mrs. Haddock

At that moment a middle-aged French gentleman sat down in the vacant place at the Haddock table.

His first act was to pick up his napkin and scrub his top plate vigorously. The three Haddocks immediately did the same. The stranger then blew his nose rather violently and the Haddocks followed suit. Then he removed his gloves.

"Ah," said Mr. Haddock pointing to his bare hands with a gesture of regret, "you have us there." And, as the stranger did not seem to understand, Mr. Haddock explained, "you have," "us," and "there" in pantomime.

"You—are—Americans—yes?" said the gentleman very slowly.

So Mr. Haddock, choosing only easy English words, answered equally slowly: "Yes."

"You — like — France — yes?" said the stranger.

"Ah," said Mr. Haddock, "we adore France."

"But you do not find Indians here, no," said the stranger.

"Very few," said Mr. Haddock, "and we miss them terribly."

"And buffaloes, no."

"No buffaloes, alas!" said Mr. Haddock, glancing longingly out of the window. But there was nothing to be seen except houses and fields, with tall trees in the distance. "No buffaloes," and he sighed nostalgically.

"You are a millionaire, yes?" asked the stranger.

Mr. Haddock brushed away an imaginary diamond which had lit on his nose.

"Oui," he replied.

"Why, Will Haddock ——!" began his wife.

Just then the waiter arrived and deposited on each plate some butter, two radishes, three olives, a sardine and a stalk of celery.

"Ah," said Mr. Haddock, "something from Congress to encourage gardening."

The *hors-d'œuvre* (for it was she) was followed by an omelette. Mr. Haddock looked at his watch.

"If this is breakfast," he said, "I should have drunk a glass of hot water before I started."

"It can't be breakfast," objected Mrs. Haddock, "it's almost twelve."

"A pretty serious problem, though," mused Mr. Haddock, and to a passing waiter he said, "Is this breakfast or lunch?"

"*Oui*, monsieur," replied the waiter.

"Breakfast or lunch?" asked Mr. Haddock.

"*Oui*, monsieur.

"Thanks," replied Mr. Haddock, and to his wife, "I think we're going to like this country."

After the omelette came another plate, and then the Haddocks were served some green string beans.

"It's a pity the cook couldn't have got everything ready at once," said Mrs. Haddock. "I suppose something is wrong with the stove."

"Maybe it's a competition," suggested Mr. Haddock. "Each cook does one dish and the winner gets Thursday night off in Paris."

"Do you suppose we really are going to Paris?" asked Mr. Haddock. "That Englishman seemed quite sure that we weren't."

They were interrupted by another waiter carrying several bottles in his hands. The man said something to Mr. Haddock in French and Mildred translated.

"He wants to know," she explained, "what you want to drink."

"I would like a glass of water, Will," said Mrs. Haddock.

So Mildred asked for that.

"He wants to know," she said, after a somewhat lengthy conversation, "what kind of water."

"Drinking water," said Mrs. Haddock.

"What name?" asked Mildred.

"Haddock," replied Mr. Haddock and he gave the waiter one of his cards. "I'm in the lumber business."

"He means," interpreted Mildred, "what name of water."

"What are some good water names?" asked Mr. Haddock.

The waiter had evidently become impatient.

"Evian," he replied, in answer to Mildred's French. "Vichy. Perrier. Vittel."

"What's that mean?" asked Mr. Haddock.

"It's the name of a water," replied Mildred.

"Vittel?" repeated Mr. Haddock. "Vittel?" and he turned to his wife. "Do you know any waters named Vittel?"

Mrs. Haddock shook her head thirstily.

"What's the first name?" asked Mr. Haddock.

The waiter, by way of reply, muttered something in French, opened three bottles, placed them on the table and moved on.

Mr. Haddock picked up the bottle in front of him.

"It seems a little yellow for water," was his remark. He looked at the label.

"Barsac," he read and poured some of it into a glass.

Mrs. Haddock did the same with hers.

"Mine's dark red," she announced, "and the name of it is 'Medoc.'"

"This water problem is going to be interesting," remarked Mr. Haddock, "when we try to take a bath."

"The French don't bathe," said Mildred. "They use perfume."

"Sh-h-h!" said her mother, with a side-long glance at the stranger.

"Well," said Mr. Haddock, "here goes." And he took a long drink from his glass. Then he looked at his daughter.

"What was the name of this water?" he asked.

"Vittel," she replied.

"Remember that name, Mildred," ordered her father and he took out his notebook and wrote the word in it. "How's yours taste, Hattie?" he asked his wife.

Mrs. Haddock sipped cautiously.

"Will," she announced, "that's not water."

"To say that," remarked Mr. Haddock, "is to criticize our daughter's French," and he patted Mildred on the head and poured out another drink for himself.

Mrs. Haddock, however, reached over and removed the extra bottle from in front of the little girl. Mildred's vigorous yell of protest was interrupted by the arrival of another

[23]

waiter with a large platter of roast veal and browned potatoes, from which he generously helped all four.

Mr. Haddock regarded his plate in dismay. "Is this all part of that same lunch?" he asked.

Nobody answered and they sat watching the Frenchman enjoy his meal as only a Frenchman can.

"At home," remarked Mildred, during one of the silences, "I am not allowed to sop up gravy with a piece of bread."

"Hush," said her father, and in order that the French gentleman might not be annoyed, he took a small piece of bread himself in his hand and began likewise to rub it around in his plate. Mildred happily followed suit and Mrs. Haddock heaved a deep sigh.

"If your grandfather," she said, "could see you now."

Mr. Haddock finished with a flourish and rubbed his fingers.

"Her grandfather," he said, "lived a very

narrow life. He never traveled. Travel," he added, "broadens one."

Mrs. Haddock fanned herself with the menu card.

"It's awfully hot in here," she remarked.

The stranger had finished with his plate and looked up. "That—is—caused—by—the—sun," he said.

"Well, well," said little Mildred, "live and learn."

The waiter arrived with a bowl of salad. The French gentleman was the only one who accepted any. After the salad, he had some cheese and a few crackers.

"I don't think I'll wait for coffee, Will," said Mrs. Haddock, giving up the fight, and she and Mildred excused themselves and left.

The next item on the menu was a basket containing fruit and a number of small, round, green things which looked a little like hard peaches. Mr. Haddock watched curiously as the gentleman opened several of these, extracted the nuts from the center, and ate them. "Almonds," he explained.

"Of course they are," said Mr. Haddock and he tried one with a certain amount of success.

"This is your first trip to Paris?" asked the stranger. Mr. Haddock nodded in the affirmative. "Paris, it is a wonderful city," said the man.

"That is what they tell me," said Mr. Haddock. "I'm looking forward to seeing it."

"The most wonderful city in the world," went on the stranger, and then he sighed and added, "but it is not Paris any longer. No. It is too full of Americans."

"An interesting criticism," remarked Mr. Haddock.

"They are everywhere," bewailed the Frenchman, "in the Bois—on the boulevards—in the cafés."

"I know just how you feel," said Mr. Haddock sympathetically.

They were interrupted by a waiter carrying an armful of various liqueurs.

"Will you have one on me?" asked Mr. Haddock.

The Frenchman hesitated a moment and then accepted. "A Grande Marnier," he said.

"The same," said Mr. Haddock and the two liqueurs were served.

"We were speaking of Paris," said Mr. Haddock.

The Frenchman shook his head sadly. "Paris is no longer Paris," he muttered.

"It's the Americans," said Mr. Haddock.

The stranger sipped his liqueur. "They are everywhere," he remarked sadly.

"It's terrible," agreed Mr. Haddock.

The Frenchman silently finished his drink.

"Will you have another?" suggested Mr. Haddock.

The Frenchman hesitated a minute and then accepted, and his glass was refilled.

"They tell me, though," said Mr. Haddock, "that you can still see some interesting things in Paris." He looked around the dining car cautiously and then lowered his voice and said, "They say that the women there are kind of different."

The Frenchman surveyed his liqueur gloomily. "Paris," he said, "isn't Paris—any ——"

"Longer," suggested Mr. Haddock, who was looking over the bill which had just been presented him by the dining car conductor. "Would you mind," he asked of his friend, "telling me what this is all about?"

The Frenchman looked at the bill and explained it to Mr. Haddock in a manner which had centuries of civilization behind it.

"Thank you," said Mr. Haddock as he paid. "And I do wish that you would take a cigar, too. My knowledge of French customs is so limited and yours," he added, "is such an old country and we have so much to learn."

The Frenchman hesitated for a minute and then accepted the cigar.

"Would you mind," apologized Mr. Haddock, rising, "if I left now? I think I'll see how my wife and daughter are making out." And with a handshake and a smile he went, leaving the Frenchman thoughtfully smoking his cigar and frugally sipping his liqueur.

CHAPTER II

MR. HADDOCK found Mrs. Haddock and little Mildred busily studying a guidebook. The nice lady from New York had not returned and the Englishman and his wife had also disappeared.

"They've gone?" asked Mr. Haddock.

"Yes," replied Mrs. Haddock, "they've gone."

"I insulted them," said Mildred with a happy smile.

Mrs. Haddock explained. "Mildred sang," she said.

"Sang what?" asked Mr. Haddock.

"It was a song I made up," said little Mildred, and then she added, "It was about England and America. Would you like to hear it?"

"No," said her father kindly.

[29]

"It was really not very nice for Mildred to do," said Mrs. Haddock.

"I'm sure it wasn't," said Mr. Haddock and he gave the little girl a new crisp fifty-franc note as a mild reproof, for little Mildred was being brought up more or less under the Montessori method.

Mrs. Haddock glanced despairingly at the various guidebooks spread out on her knees. "It's going to be rather hard, Will," she said, "to do all of Paris in four days."

"Mrs. Jenkins did," said Mr. Haddock, firmly. "And what a Jenkins did, a Haddock can do. We'll begin by making a complete schedule for each day," and he took out his notebook and wrote *"Tuesday."*

"But we arrive this afternoon," said Mrs. Haddock, "and we can probably see a lot of things still to-day."

"All right," said Mr. Haddock and he changed *"Tuesday"* to *"Monday."*

"First," said Mrs. Haddock, "we'll go to the hotel and get washed up."

"Baths," said Mr. Haddock gleefully.

"Why?" asked little Mildred.

"Because," replied her father.

"And then," went on Mrs. Haddock, "we could go to the Louvre."

So after *"Bath,"* Mr. Haddock more or less wrote *"Louvre."*

"How long do you think that ought to take?" asked Mrs. Haddock.

Mr. Haddock reached for the guidebook. "It looks pretty large," he said, "from the picture. Do we want to go inside?"

"Of course," replied Mrs. Haddock; "that's where the Mona Lisa is."

"It oughtn't to take long," said Mr. Haddock, "to look at the Mona Lisa. How big a picture is it?"

"We are going," said Mrs. Haddock, "to look at every picture in the Louvre. Mrs. Jenkins did."

Mr. Haddock once more picked up the guidebook. "Gosh!" he said, and with his pencil he did some figuring for several minutes on the margin of one of the pages. "Allowing," he finally said, "for wind and unfavorable weather conditions, we can possibly get through with the Louvre about five o'clock next Friday morning. And I'm not sure," he added, "that they would let us sleep there all those nights, either."

There was a moment's dismay at this announcement.

"Let me see the book," said Mrs. Haddock.

"We might start with something easier," suggested her husband, "like Napoleon's tomb or the Bastille."

"That ought to be pretty easy," sneered little Mildred, "because there isn't any Bastille."

"Mildred," said her father, "papa didn't bring you three thousand miles to have you make critical remarks."

Mrs. Haddock looked up from the guide-book. "We might," she suggested, "pass through some of the rooms of the Louvre rather quickly."

"On roller skates," suggested her husband. "That would save quite a bit of time. Did you pack our roller skates?"

Mrs. Haddock shook her head.

"Well, then, the thing to do," said Mr. Haddock, "is to select the best pictures and look only at those."

"Mrs. Jenkins," observed Mrs. Haddock, "looked at every one."

"Does that include the frames, too?" asked her husband.

Mrs. Haddock shook her head, and did not reply.

"Well, anyway," said Mr. Haddock, "let's leave that undecided. Now what shall we do to-morrow?" and he wrote *"Tuesday"* again on his list. "First," he suggested, "breakfast. Where shall we have breakfast?"

"In the hotel dining room," replied Mrs. Haddock, "of course."

"All right," said Mr. Haddock, "and then?"

"Then," said Mrs. Haddock, glancing through the guidebook, "Père Lachaise Cemetery."

"Isn't that a little soon," objected Mr. Haddock, "after breakfast?"

[33]

"Not if you eat plenty of vegetables," said little Mildred, with a giggle.

Mrs. Haddock looked out the window as the train rushed past another station. "I think we're getting near Paris," she said.

"How long should we allow for Père Lachaise?" asked Mr. Haddock, pencil poised in air.

"Half an hour," said Mrs. Haddock.

"And then?"

"The Bois de Boulogne."

"What's there to look at?" asked Mr. Haddock.

"Trees," replied his wife.

"We didn't come all this way," objected Mr. Haddock, "to look at trees."

"French trees are different," said Mrs. Haddock.

Her husband glanced out of the window. "All right," he said, "we'll go to the Bois. Then where?"

"Notre Dame," said Mrs. Haddock.

"Good," replied her husband. "How long there?"

Mrs. Haddock consulted the guidebook. "Half an hour," she said.

"Doing what?" asked Mr. Haddock.

"You go up in one of the towers," said Mrs. Haddock, "and that probably takes a little time."

"If there is an elevator," said Mr. Haddock, "it oughtn't to be so long. Call it twenty minutes."

"All right," said Mrs. Haddock, "and then the Sewers."

"Now you're talking," said Mr. Haddock. "It's been a long time since I've seen a good sewer."

"And after the Sewers," said Mrs. Haddock.

"Lunch," said Mr. Haddock.

Little Mildred laughed. "And *vice versa*," she said.

Just then the lady from New York, who had evidently been in hiding in another compartment, reappeared at the door. "We're almost there," she said.

"Good," said Mr. Haddock. "We were

just sort of planning a schedule of what to do. How does this sound?" and he read her their proposed itinerary.

The lady smiled. "The Louvre is closed on Monday," she said.

"Then *that* problem is solved," said Mr. Haddock.

"And I don't think," went on the lady, "that they let people go through the Sewers any more without special permission."

"You're quite a help," said Mr. Haddock. "Is there anything wrong with Notre Dame?"

"Only your pronunciation of it," sneered little Mildred.

"Ah," said Mr. Haddock, chucking her under the chin, "you French."

"And really," said the lady, "you must be sure to go see the Sainte-Chapelle."

"All right," said Mr. Haddock, "we'll go there instead of the Sewers."

The towns through which the train was speeding became more and more numerous and closer and closer together. The advertisements for things called "Dubonnet" and

"Byrrh" and "Cointreau" began to appear on more and more houses. Other trains were passed which were evidently for suburban traffic; on top of several of the coaches there were places where people—French people— were sitting under awnings and reading newspapers.

"It's sort of exciting," said Mr. Haddock as the train went whizzing past a number of curious looking wooden box cars which Mr. Haddock had seen before only in war pictures. Indeed, the war suddenly seemed very near, the war which Mr. Haddock had always thought of as something very, very far away. The faces of the men on the station platforms seemed exactly like the newspaper faces of French soldiers, and occasionally there were to be seen men who were actually dressed in the light-blue uniform.

"Gosh!" said Mr. Haddock, and he looked at his wife. She, however, was busy putting the guidebook back in the suitcase.

"I've often wondered what it was like," said Mr. Haddock to the lady. "Paris."

"Paris," said the lady, shaking her head, "isn't Paris any more."

"I know," said Mr. Haddock with just the trace of a glint in his eye. "The Americans have spoiled it."

The train rushed on over bridges and past embankments. Mrs. Haddock finished packing the bags and began looking for Mildred's gloves. A sign, "Paris 500 KM," flashed by. Streets and houses were above them, tracks spread out in all directions around them. Then two more bridges and the train began to slow down. Mr. Haddock took out his handkerchief and wiped the palms of his hands, then looked at the lady to see if he could help her with her baggage. She, too, was excited; her eyes were shining brightly and she was breathing rather quickly and nervously. Mildred was twisting her hands together in her lap and only Mrs. Haddock was calm.

"I hope there will be porters, Will," she said.

The train slowed, gave one or two slight jerks, went ahead again, then gradually and

quietly slid over the rails into the station.
Paris.

"This arrival will be a great disappointment
to that Englishman," said Mr. Haddock as he
reached for his suitcase.

The porter took Mr. Haddock's baggage
through the window, passed a strap through
the handles of the bags, threw them over his
shoulder and started down the long platform
toward the distant gate. The Haddocks followed.

It was all a little confusing. People were
running in both directions, stopping, exclaim-
ing, and embracing. The train had emptied
very quickly. Two platforms away another
train was just leaving and men in uniform
were running along, shutting doors and blow-
ing whistles.

"Did you get the number of that porter?"
asked Mrs. Haddock. Mr. Haddock shook
his head. "Did he give you a receipt?" asked
his wife.

Mr. Haddock felt in all his pockets. "No,"

[39]

he said, "and look, the conductor never took our tickets."

This latter fact somewhat reassured Mr. Haddock. Any country in which the railroads were so inefficient as to let passengers ride without collecting their tickets was certainly not a country to be greatly feared, and with a gesture of contempt Mr. Haddock tossed the useless tickets away.

There was quite a crowd trying to get out the narrow gate and Mr. Haddock recognized and spoke to many of his acquaintances of the steamship. "So this is Paris," said five or ten, possibly fifteen, and each time Mr. Haddock laughed and agreed that it was.

By the time they reached the narrow exit, however, he was beginning to be a little bit irritated, for Mr. Haddock didn't like crowds very well, especially when he had Mrs. Haddock and Mildred to take care of, and it was with a sigh of relief that he reached the gate and started through.

He didn't get through. He was stopped by a man in uniform who evidently wanted something from him. Mr. Haddock showed the man his passport, but it wasn't that. "Maybe it's some sort of a medical examination," said Mrs. Haddock, so Mr. Haddock showed the man his tongue. But it wasn't that either, and the man began to be a little menacing in his demand. Mildred came to the rescue. "He wants your tickets," she said.

"What tickets?" asked Mr. Haddock.

"Your railroad tickets," said little Mildred.

"Why, the idea!" said Mrs. Haddock.

Mr. Haddock by this time was becoming quite a little worried. "Tell him," he said, "that in America ——"

Just then a gentleman in uniform, with "American Express Company" on his hat, stepped up, said something to the gateman, and the Haddocks were allowed to pass through. Mr. Haddock was very grateful; Mrs. Haddock, however, continued to be quite indignant. "This is certainly a funny country," she said.

The American Express gentleman smiled sympathetically.

"Where did you want to go?" he asked.

Mrs. Haddock surveyed him suspiciously.

"We're quite able to take care of ourselves, thank you," she replied and, taking Mildred by the hand, she walked away toward the outer exit.

Mr. Haddock, somewhat apologetic, held out his hand to the gentleman.

"Women are funny, like that," he said.

"Women," replied the other, "are the riddle of the universe."

"Yes," said Mr. Haddock, "that's right."

"A woman's smile," said the American Express man, "is the gateway to heaven and the doorway to hell."

"Yes," said Mr. Haddock, shifting somewhat uneasily on his feet, "but ——"

"In a woman's eyes ——" began the American Express man.

"You're right," agreed Mr. Haddock again, "and could you tell me where I could get a taxicab?"

"Right over there," said the gentleman,

OFF THEY DROVE IN THE CUSTODY OF THAT SINISTER-
LOOKING DRIVER

pointing, and Mr. Haddock shook hands again and left.

In the large hall Mr. Haddock found his wife, his daughter, and his baggage, and they followed the porter down a wide, long flight of stairs and out into the streets of Paris.

As they emerged Mr. Haddock was suddenly and completely deafened. He had never in his life heard so many automobile horns at one time. Bewildered, he felt himself piled into an open taxicab with a strange sloping hood over the engine; he fumbled nervously and gave the porter all the francs he had, and then in a minute, off they drove in the custody of that sinister-looking driver with a dirty linen duster and a mustache.

And at the end of five minutes Mr. Haddock looked at his wife. She was sitting there, pale but determined. Mr. Haddock leaned over and whispered: "He's gone mad. I've heard of cases like that. If he ever slows down, you hit him over the head and I'll grab the wheel." But the driver didn't slow down. He went faster.

Little Mildred, however, was evidently having the time of her life.

"We just missed that last street car," she announced, happily, "by an inch."

There seemed to be millions of other taxicabs all going just as fast and all honking just as loudly. There were hundreds of great auto busses tearing along at break-neck speed. There were pedestrians and sidewalk cafés with people sitting in them and drinking just like Mr. Haddock had read about—and then suddenly they dashed across a street into a passageway under a large stone building and came out into the biggest garden of the most beautiful flowers Mr. Haddock had ever seen. The cab swung to the right and Mr. Haddock looked around.

"Gosh!" he said.

The immense flower bed was inclosed on three sides by the old dark gray walls of a long building and Mr. Haddock suddenly realized.

"It's the Louvre," he said.

"Of course," said little Mildred, "and these are the Tuileries Gardens and off there is the

Place de la Concorde. And look, way, way, in the distance you can see the Arc de Triomphe."

"Don't point," said Mrs. Haddock.

"And statues," said Mr. Haddock, "all over the place."

"Naked women," said little Mildred.

"And geraniums," said Mr. Haddock. "Why, this must have cost a fortune."

They passed through the archway at the other side, across another street, and on to a bridge.

"The Seine," said little Mildred, "and there is Notre Dame down there to the left."

"And the Eiffel Tower," said Mr. Haddock, pointing to the right. "Oh, gosh! Hattie. How about it?"

Mrs. Haddock did not answer. "Do you think he knows the right way?" she said.

Across the Seine they dashed into a narrow street where the noise of their horn became almost deafening. And then, after a while, they pulled up in front of a hotel.

CHAPTER III

THE Hôtel de New York et Sainte-Agnes. All three sat there for a moment while the chauffeur climbed down and began unloading their bags.

"That's the last time," said Mrs. Haddock, "that I ride in a taxicab in Paris."

"But, Hattie ——" began her husband, and then he stopped and smiled. "All right, dear," he said. He looked at the sign outside the door of the hotel: *"Dernier Confort."*

"What's that mean?" he asked Mildred.

"Last Comfort," she replied.

"That sounds like something a priest gives you," said Mr. Haddock, a little worried.

"After a taxicab ride," added Mrs. Haddock grimly.

A man in a blue frock coat and an official looking cap came out of the door of the hotel followed by a servant wearing a black leather apron. The servant picked up the bags and carried them in. Mr. Haddock paid the taxi bill and they followed the frock-coated gentleman into the hotel.

"I would like," said Mr. Haddock to an old lady in black who was sitting behind a desk —"I would like two rooms with a connecting bath."

The lady smiled mirthlessly and bowed and said something to the servant.

"Will you get into the lift, please?" she said, and pointed to what looked like a telephone booth.

"Will I get into what?" asked Mr. Haddock.

"The lift," replied the lady, "the *ascenseur*."

"Elevator," translated Mildred.

The servant pulled the two doors open. Mr. and Mrs. Haddock and Mildred stepped in, the doors were closed, the iron gate was slammed shut, the servant on the outside pressed a button, and the Haddocks, all alone and squeezed tightly together, found them-

[47]

selves starting jerkily upward. It was a terrifying moment in their lives.

"Well, anyway, dear," said Mr. Haddock, "it's slower than that taxicab."

"It's slower than anything I've ever seen," said Mrs. Haddock.

They reached and passed something marked "Entresol" and then a floor marked "1ᵉʳ Étage."

"First floor," said little Mildred.

"Well, we're not losing any," remarked her father. "That's something."

In another ten minutes the second floor was reached.

"Well," said Mr. Haddock, taking out his daily schedule, "we don't need to worry any more about the rest of this afternoon," and under *"Monday"* he wrote *"Elevator."* "I wonder," he added, "if there is a dining car attached."

"Oh dear! Will," said Mrs. Haddock, "I wish it would hurry."

At the third floor the elevator unexpectedly stopped. The servant opened the door and the Haddocks emerged.

"Have you been waiting long?" asked Mr. Haddock.

The man shook his head dumbly.

"Next time," said Mr. Haddock, "we'll come up by way of the canal."

The man closed the elevator door, pressed a button, and the car slowly descended.

"Ask him," said Mr. Haddock of Mildred, "if they have the same time down there as we have up here," and he made as though to set his watch an hour ahead.

Mildred laughed. The servant beckoned and they followed him down a corridor and into a room.

It was a large room and quite unlike that of any hotel Mr. Haddock had ever visited. The walls were papered in bright red and Mrs. Haddock glanced suspiciously at one or two of the pictures. The bed was quite large, and although there was no clothes closet, there was a big old-fashioned wardrobe and some quite uncomfortable-looking chairs. Mrs. Haddock felt of the bed and, when the man wasn't looking, quickly turned back one of the sheets and glanced inside, but with no luck.

"Bath?" she asked.

Mildred translated, and the man showed them a small room containing a washstand, a mirror, and a few shelves.

"Yes," said Mr. Haddock, "but where do you take a bath?"

The man pointed, and under the washstand Mr. Haddock observed a white porcelain object of an unknown shape. The general outline was that of a figure "8."

"The last people who had this room," said Mr. Haddock, "must have been Singer's midgets. Ask him if there isn't a real large, American bathtub somewhere."

The servant nodded and they followed him out into the hall, at the end of which there was a room marked "Salle de Bain," and there they discovered a bathtub.

"But," objected Mr. Haddock, "we wanted two rooms with connecting bath."

The servant shrugged his shoulders and informed Mildred that such a thing was, unfortunately, impossible.

"All right," said Mr. Haddock. "Let's see the other room, then—the one that connects with ours."

The connecting room was quite similar to the one they had just seen and the Haddocks went into conference. Mrs. Haddock spoke for five minutes on the negative, bringing out in her inimitable way that the rooms did not look clean, that the beds seemed very hard and unsafe, and that the servant had on a dirty apron.

Mr. Haddock, speaking for the affirmative, began by telling a story about the man who asked the Irishman if he had ever played a violin. He was not allowed, however, to finish the story, and so, in answer to his opponent's direct question, he replied that as long as they were in the hotel they might as well stay there, and that as far as he was concerned, it didn't look dirty to him and, besides, what did Mrs. Haddock expect to find in the Old World— the Statler? He concluded with a magnificent plea for toleration and better understanding between the two great nations and sat down amid what might be termed a round of applause from his daughter Mildred.

In rebuttal, Mrs. Haddock repeated her three major premises, declaring that Mr. Haddock had in no way replied to any of them and ended by saying that all men are alike and asking Mr. Haddock what he would do in case of a fire or something.

"In case of a fire or something," replied Mr. Haddock, "my first thought would be of my wife and child."

"Fiddlesticks!" replied Mrs. Haddock.

"And as for your insinuation that men are all alike, I can only point to the third verse of the second chapter of the Gospel according to —"

"All right, Will," said Mrs. Haddock, "we'll stay."

"Goody!" said Mr. Haddock, and he gave orders for the baggage to be brought up to their rooms.

After the man had gone, Mr. Haddock

walked to the window and looked out. There was a good deal of traffic going on in the street below and a great deal of noise from the horns of the passing automobiles.

"Well, Hattie," he said, "we're in Paris."

"It will probably get quieter at night," said Mrs. Haddock, also looking out. "And, Will, I wish you would arrange for a bath."

Mr. Haddock walked over to the wall and surveyed three push buttons—one marked "Valet de Chambre," another "Femme de Chambre," and the third "Sommelier."

"Do any of those words," he asked his daughter, "mean 'bath'?"

She shook her head. "Press all three," suggested Mildred, "and see what happens."

"I wouldn't do that," said Mrs. Haddock. "One of them might be for fire."

"Have you any objection," asked Mr. Haddock, reprovingly, "to firemen?"

Mrs. Haddock did not reply.

"I'll tell you what," said little Mildred, "we'll put a little sugar on each button and the one a fly lights on first, we'll press, and maybe we'll get a bath."

"Good," said Mr. Haddock. "And would you like to place a little bet on the side?"

"Now don't go gambling again, Will," said Mrs. Haddock. "I don't want Mildred to gamble, either."

"I'm not gambling," said little Mildred. "I know flies from A to Z."

Mr. Haddock laughed. "Would you like to make it thirty francs?" he asked. Mildred shook her head.

"Ten francs," she said, "and I would like to have you put up the money before we start."

"That's very unkind of you, Mildred," said Mr. Haddock. "You'll be sorry—some day—when I'm gone."

"Don't joke about those things, Will," said Mrs. Haddock.

Mr. Haddock took a lump of sugar out of his pocket and began smearing it on the three push buttons.

"Now," he said, "where are the flies?"

"There aren't any," said little Mildred, "but we can ring for some."

"Yes," said Mr. Haddock. "And which button would *that* be?"

"This one," said Mildred, and she pressed "Sommelier."

"If I'd only studied French," said Mr. Haddock, regretfully.

"Here's a fly," cried little Mildred, excitedly, and father and daughter watched eagerly while the little "fellow" flew several times around the room.

"There he goes," said Mr. Haddock, and they watched breathlessly as he (or she) neared the three push buttons. Then, hesitating for a moment, it circled once more and flew out of the window.

"Maybe that isn't the right kind of sugar," said Mr. Haddock. "We forgot, didn't we, that it was a French fly?"

"There's a chance here," said little Mildred, "for some sort of a joke about Spanish fly, but I can't seem to get it worked in."

A knock came on the door.

"Come in," said Mr. Haddock.

The knock was repeated.

"Entrez," said Mildred, with just a suggestion of a superior smile.

The door opened and the *sommelier* appeared. He was dressed a good deal like a waiter; in fact, he was dressed exactly like a waiter, although it was then only three in the afternoon.

"You can't ask a man in evening clothes," whispered Mr. Haddock, aside, "for a bath— or can you?"

"Sure you can," said little Mildred. "The French are different. You can ask them anything."

"All right," said Mr. Haddock. "Ask him how he got that spot on his shirt."

"It's not my shirt," said the *sommelier* . . . unexpectedly.

"Oh, I beg your pardon!" said Mr. Haddock. "I didn't know you were English."

"I'm not English," said the *sommelier*.

"Then what are you?" said Mr. Haddock.

"And whose shirt is that?" asked little Mildred.

The *sommelier* closed the door. "Would you like to hear my story?" he asked.

"If it's interesting," said little Mildred.

The *sommelier* cleared his throat and began.

"We were three brothers ———"

"Who were three brothers?" asked little Mildred.

The *sommelier* looked at Mr. Haddock. "I can't tell this story," he said, "if that little girl is going to interrupt me all the time."

"She won't," said Mr. Haddock, and he gave his daughter a look signifying "she won't."

"We were there brothers," said the *sommelier,* "and then the war came."

"What war?" asked little Mildred.

"The Great War," replied the *sommelier,* and he said nothing for a moment in an attempt to control his emotion.

"There, there, my good fellow!" said Mr. Haddock, encouragingly.

"As you know," went on the *sommelier* at last, "Germany and Austria had been planning and plotting for years to destroy the peace of Europe. In August, 1914, their long-awaited opportunity came. The Archduke Ferdinand was assassinated in Sarajevo on June 29th, as you remember ——"

"Twenty-eighth," corrected little Mildred.

"Twenty-eighth," repeated the *sommelier*. "And the match was thrown into the powder magazine, whence who could foretell the outcome. On August 1st came the ultimatum to Russia; on August 2d German troops crossed over into French territory. On August 3d war was declared. And my country—my country—brave little Belgium ——"

Tears were streaming down his face.

"Ah," he cried, "you Americans, you forget so easily—you are so rich, so prosperous ——"

He was silent.

Mr. Haddock walked over and shook him by the hand.

"No," said Mr. Haddock, "you are wrong. We have not forgotten. We will never forget." And he took out his pocketbook and gave the man five hundred francs.

"Thank you, sir," said the man, glancing first at the amount. "Was there anything else?"

"A bath," replied Mr. Haddock. "But don't mind about that now."

The *sommelier* bowed. "I'll send you the *valet de chambre*." And putting the money carefully in his pocket, he withdrew.

Mr. Haddock walked to the window and looked out. "They *have* been through an awful lot over here," he said.

A knock came at the door.

"*Entrez*," said Mr. Haddock before Mildred could speak. It was the *valet de chambre*.

"You wish something?" he said.

"Ah," said Mr. Haddock. "You speak English, too?"

The man nodded. "I am a Belgian," he said, simply, and he closed the door behind him. "We were five brothers—and then the war came. Ah," he said, clenching his fists, "those terrible German hordes pouring down upon our brave little country. Ah," he cried, "those never-ending lines in their field-gray uniforms, those helmets, those cannons. Yes," he cried, "and for a moment civilization wavered."

"That's from the *Four Horsemen of the Apocalypse*," said little Mildred, "about page seventy-three."

The valet bit his lip and continued: "My brothers and I were called to the colors. I think," he said, dropping his hands to his sides, "you know the rest."

"Yes," said Mr. Haddock, "I think I do." And taking a five-hundred-franc note from his pocket, he gave it to the man, who withdrew with a bow. "This is getting to be the most expensive bath I have almost ever taken," said Mr. Haddock.

A rap came on the door. It was the *femme de chambre*. "You wish a bath?" she said.

"Yes," replied Mr. Haddock.

"By any chance," asked little Mildred, "are you a Belgian?"

The maid closed the door. "We were seven sisters ——"

"Will Haddock," said Mrs. Haddock, "if you give this woman a cent ——"

"But think," said Mr. Haddock, tears in his eyes, "of brave little Belgium."

"I'm thinking," said little Mildred.

"I'm thinking, too," said Mrs. Haddock. "I'm thinking that I'm hot and tired and I would like a bath!"

"But, monsieur," said the maid, looking at Mr. Haddock appealingly.

"A bath," said Mrs. Haddock, "in a bath-tub. Now!"

"*Oui*, madame," said the maid, and with a smile at Mr. Haddock she bowed and with drew.

Mr. Haddock began to whistle a tune.

"Will Haddock," said Mrs. Haddock, "you're a fool!"

"Why, my dear?" asked her husband. "Just because I want to do something in the cause of humanity? Just because I want to hold high the torch of ——"

[61]

"If I see you talking with that maid again," said Mrs. Haddock, "we leave this hotel."

"Yes, ma'am," said Mr. Haddock.

"Incidentally," said little Mildred, "who gets the first bath?"

"Why, your mother, of course!" said Mr. Haddock.

"And then?" asked the little girl.

Her father laughed. "I'll give you two guesses," he said.

"Me," said little Mildred.

"Guess again," said her father.

"You," said little Mildred.

Mr. Haddock began removing his collar.

"I tell you what," said little Mildred. "The first one who gets undressed gets the bath."

"The bath immediately following your mother's," said Mr. Haddock, "is to be taken by a Mr. William Haddock of Legion, Ohio." And he started to remove his shoes.

"That is little short of tyranny," said Mildred, "and I would not be surprised if I ran away to sea."

"I'd be glad to help you," said her father, "pick out a good boat."

Mrs. Haddock had gone into the next room and now reappeared in a kimono.

"Mildred," announced Mr. Haddock, "is going to run away to sea."

"She'll do nothing of the sort," said Mrs. Haddock.

"Oh, shoot!" said the little girl. "You never let me do anything."

There was another knock on the door. It was the *femme de chambre* again and she said something to Mildred in French, at which the little girl laughed very loudly.

"Well," said her father, "what is it?"

"There isn't any hot water," she announced happily.

Mr. Haddock regarded his daughter for several minutes in silence, then he slowly began drawing on his shoes again. The maid had retired and Mrs. Haddock was grimly unpacking the suitcases.

"Well," said Mr. Haddock, "a lot of people have died in bathtubs."

"Not in French bathtubs," said Mrs. Haddock.

Mr. Haddock took out his watch from the coat hanging over the back of a chair.

"It's half-past three," he said. "Don't you think it would be nice to take a ride?"

"Where?" asked Mrs. Haddock.

"Oh, just around Paris."

"Swell," cried little Mildred and she began putting on her hat.

Mrs. Haddock sat down determinedly on the edge of the bed. "I'll stay here," she said.

"But, Hattie ——" began Mr. Haddock.

"No," said Mrs. Haddock. "You and Mildred go. I've got lots of things to do—the unpacking, and—and cleaning up this room, and lots of things."

"But the unpacking can wait," said Mr. Haddock. "And this is our first day in Paris."

"No," she replied. "I want to see if anything in the baggage has been stolen. And besides, I want to wash my white gloves and Mildred's new stockings."

Mr. Haddock glanced at his wife for a minute, then pulled on his coat and reached for his hat. "Come on, Mildred," he said, and taking his daughter by the hand, they started out.

"Don't let Mildred eat anything," called Mrs. Haddock after them.

When they reached the elevator cage, Mr. Haddock pressed the button and they waited. After ten minutes he tried again. Nothing happened.

"It's lucky," said Mr. Haddock, "that we're not in a hurry."

"But I am," said little Mildred. "I want to get out. I want to see Paris."

"So do I," said Mr. Haddock, and he pushed the button once more. "Maybe there's an express elevator somewhere," he said.

Mildred turned and asked a question in French of a chambermaid who was passing in the corridor with a handful of keys. The maid replied and Mildred took her father's hand and they started to walk downstairs.

"She says," explained little Mildred, "it's a one-way elevator."

"That's quite an improvement," said Mr.

Haddock, "on the old two-way type. I shouldn't be surprised," he added, "if some day, in the not too far distant future, the French will invent some marvelous instrument by means of which a person can sit right here in Paris and talk to somebody half a mile away."

"Yes," said little Mildred. "And I know a good name for it."

"What?" asked her father.

"The telephone!" cried little Mildred.

"Shhh!" said her father. "They might burn us as witches."

They passed out into the street and turned to the left.

"And besides," he added, "mere speed isn't progress. With all our modern inventions, are we any happier?"

"I am," said little Mildred. "I'm having a swell time."

Mr. Haddock regarded his daughter curiously. "I wish your mother was," he said.

They hailed a taxi.

"Tell him," said Mr. Haddock, "to take us around Paris. France," he added.

They got in, and the taxi started. In a minute or two, they were at the Seine, and this time, instead of crossing, the driver turned to the left and drove along the *quai*.

"That's the Louvre again over there," explained little Mildred, "on the right bank."

"And look at those barges," said her father, excitedly, "and that little steamboat—*La Belle Jardinière*."

Mildred corrected his pronunciation patiently.

"And this is the Chamber of Deputies," she announced. "You aren't looking."

"Yes, I am," said her father. "And there is the Eiffel Tower ahead. Gosh! it's tall, isn't it?"

"Nine hundred and eighty-four feet," said little Mildred.

"I bet it isn't as tall as the Woolworth Building, though," said her father.

"Yes, it is," said little Mildred. "The

Woolworth Building is seven hundred and fifty feet high."

"Well, I bet it didn't cost as much," said Mr. Haddock.

"The cost of it is at present unknown," said little Mildred, "but it contains two million, five hundred thousand iron rivets."

"Two million, five hundred thousand and three," corrected her father. "Mrs. Jenkins counted them."

The Eiffel Tower grew larger and taller as they approached. When they were opposite the field over which its frame was hovering, the taxi driver suddenly stopped the car and said something in French.

"He says," translated Mildred, "it's the Eiffel Tower."

"My!" said her father, holding up his hands in surprise. "The Eiffel Tower. Well, well!"

The taxi driver muttered something, shrugged his shoulders, and drove on. They turned to the right, crossed the river, drove around behind a very ugly building which Mildred, after looking in the guidebook, announced was the Trocadero, and then through some comparatively quiet streets until they came, all of a sudden, upon a very large and beautiful arch.

"Don't tell me," said Mr. Haddock. "I know what *that* is."

They stopped the taxi and got out and walked slowly under. Mr. Haddock took off his hat and they joined the small group of people who were gazing in silence at the flame burning over the grave of the Unknown Soldier. One of the Americans was speaking:

"It's gas," he was saying. "There's a pipe underneath."

"I should think it would be dangerous," said one of the women, "if it blows out."

"I wonder who pays for the gas," said another. "It must cost quite a lot in a year."

Mr. Haddock took his daughter by the hand and they walked away and back to their taxicab in silence.

"Now," said Mildred, looking at the map, "we'll go down the Champs Élysées to the Place de la Concorde. And then ——"

"And then," said Mr. Haddock, "I think your father would like a nice cool drink."

As they sped along the Champs Élysées, Mr. Haddock and Mildred stood up and looked back at the Arc de Triomphe. Then they turned; ahead, in the distance, there was another arch.

"The boy who built this street," said Mr. Haddock, "knew what he was doing."

Faster and faster they raced, and then suddenly the avenue of trees opened out into the largest square Mr. Haddock had ever seen.

"The Place de la Concorde," said Mildred.

The cab swung around the circle and between two large fountains. Mildred pointed across the river.

"Over there," she said, "is the Chamber of Deputies again. And that"—and she pointed in the direction in which they were going—"is the Madeleine."

Mr. Haddock was gazing in all directions around the square. "It's an awful lot of space, isn't it," he said, "not to be used for something."

"Marie Antoinette was executed here," explained little Mildred.

"I never could see why they did that," said Mr. Haddock.

"I'll tell you some time," promised the little girl.

"And that," she added, "is an obelisk."

"Indeed!" said Mr. Haddock. "I've always wanted to see an obelisk."

They passed out of the Place into a wide street and approached the Madeleine. Then they swung to the right on to a very busy boulevard where, after a minute's driving, they were held up by the first traffic officer that Mr. Haddock had seen in two weeks.

"Look!" said Mildred. "There's the Opéra."

"So it is," said Mr. Haddock. "And there is a café."

So they paid the driver, got out, and crossed the boulevard to a large restaurant where a great many people were sitting at tables on the sidewalk.

Mr. and Mrs. Haddock

"The Café de la Paix," said Mr. Haddock, reading the awning. "Let's try this."

So they sat down. In a few minutes a waiter appeared, and in a few more minutes Mr. Haddock was raising to his lips a tall glass of beautiful cold, foamy beer.

"Say, I wish the boys could see me now," he said.

CHAPTER IV

WHEN Mr. Haddock and little Mildred returned to the hotel, they found that Mrs. Haddock had set everything in order, unpacked all the bags, and put pictures of various members of the Haddock family in different places in the room.

"Why," said Mr. Haddock, cheerfully, "it looks just like home."

Mrs. Haddock sighed. "I wonder," she said, "how soon we can get any mail."

"To-morrow," replied Mr. Haddock. "I'll go the first thing in the morning."

He looked at his watch. "It's about six o'clock," he said. "We might as well start to get ready for dinner."

"Will," said Mrs. Haddock, "let's don't go to any big place to-night. I don't feel much like dressing."

[73]

"But, Hattie," objected her husband, "don't you think we sort of ought to celebrate? It's our first night in Paris."

Mrs. Haddock shook her head. "I'm tired," she said, "and I had a big argument with that chambermaid after you left."

"Oh, come on, Hattie," said Mr. Haddock. "Let's forget our troubles. This is Paris." And he looked so eager that Mrs. Haddock finally agreed and they all began to dress.

"Now," said Mr. Haddock as they left the hotel an hour later, "where shall we go?"

"Here's a list," said little Mildred, opening the guidebook.

"Read a few names," said her father.

"Aunt Flora," suggested Mrs. Haddock, "said that the Duval Restaurants were very good—and very reasonable."

"But hang it, Hattie," said Mr. Haddock, "I don't want anything reasonable—to-night. I tell you what," he added, "we'll ask a taxi driver."

"Oh dear!" said Mrs. Haddock.

But in spite of her protests, Mr. Haddock hailed a passing cab and they got in.

"I suppose I ride backward," said little Mildred, pulling down the seat.

"You do," said Mr. Haddock. "And ask him," he continued, "to take us to the best restaurant in Paris."

After a few minutes' conversation with Mildred the driver pulled down the flag, which was marked *"Libre,"* and they started.

"I'm getting to know this town pretty well," said Mr. Haddock as they came once more to the Seine, crossed it and went again into the Tuileries Gardens.

"This is the Carrousel arch we saw in the distance," said little Mildred, "when we were coming down the Champs Élysées."

"Yes, sir, Hattie!" cried Mr. Haddock, excitedly. "And there's that Arch of Triumph I was telling you about way off there at the other end of the avenue."

The sun was setting directly behind the distant monument at which Mr. Haddock was pointing. He stopped the cab for a minute and the three Americans watched as the western sky grew crimson. The walls of the Louvre and the statues of the garden were soft in the light of the setting sun and there was a certain fragrance in the air—the fragrance of Paris. Mr. Haddock breathed deeply.

"It smells good," he said. "Paris."

On a bench near them, a young couple were kissing and making love in apparently complete disregard of the fact that it was not yet dark.

"They ought to be ashamed of themselves," said Mrs. Haddock, "in the open like that."

Mr. Haddock took his wife's hand and they sat there. Then he suddenly leaned over and kissed her on the cheek. Mrs. Haddock blushed and looked around to see if anyone was watching.

"Why, Will Haddock!" she said. "You've been drinking."

"No, he hasn't. Honest, mamma," said little Mildred. "Only two beers."

The cab drove ahead through the opposite

gates, and soon they were on the avenue at the other end of which they could see the dome-crowned roof of the Opéra. Then, in a little while, the taxi stopped, the door was opened by a gentleman in uniform, and the three Haddocks descended.

Inside they were met by a very polite woman who took their hats and coats, and by a still more polite head waiter. A *chef* near the door was cooking something on what looked like a chafing-dish, under which blue flames were burning.

The waiter pulled out a table. Mr. and Mrs. Haddock seated themselves on a cushioned bench extending the length of the wall; the table was pushed back, and little Mildred sat down in a chair opposite them. Everyone else in the room was in evening clothes, but there was no music.

"It seems sort of funny," said Mrs. Haddock, "to get all dressed up just to eat."

The waiter handed them large menu cards and Mr. Haddock, with a thrill of anticipation, began to run his eye over the various offerings. After a few minutes, however, he turned to his wife in dismay.

"I can't make much out of it, Hattie," he said.

"Neither can I," replied she, "except that the prices seem very high. Shall we go somewhere else?"

"Of course not," replied Mr. Haddock. "Mildred, will you please explain to your father, for example, what this means?" And he pointed to an item on the card.

"That," replied his daughter, "is spinach."

Mr. Haddock looked again. "Well, well!" he said. "So that's spinach," and he shook his head. "Sometimes," he said, "it seems as though I never shall learn this language. And what is that?"

"Kidneys," replied little Mildred.

"That reminds me," said Mr. Haddock, "how about starting with a cocktail of some sort?"

"None for me," said Mrs. Haddock, "and none for Mildred."

"O.K.," said Mr. Haddock, and he returned to his perusal of the menu.

"Can I help you, perhaps?" asked one of the two or three waiters who were hovering near the Haddocks' table.

"Oh," said Mr. Haddock, with a sigh of relief. "You speak English?"

"Yes, sir," replied the waiter, but without too much assurance.

"Would you mind speaking some?" asked Mr. Haddock. "Just a sentence or two, so that we can be sure."

The waiter stood up very straight, dropped his hands to his sides, and began:

"I see the ball," he said, very slowly.

"That's right," said Mr. Haddock, encouragingly. "Now, again."

The waiter took a deep breath.

"Does Alice see the ball?" he said.

"Fine," cried Mr. Haddock. "Now"—and he picked up the menu—"what's a good soup?"

The waiter pointed to an item on the card.

"All right," said Mr. Haddock. "How about three of those?"

[79]

Mrs. Haddock agreed, but little Mildred shook her head.

"I'm not very hungry," she said.

Her father and mother looked at her in surprise.

"You are not very what?" asked Mr. Haddock.

"Hungry," said the girl.

"Will," accused Mrs. Haddock, "you've been letting her stuff herself with a lot of things this afternoon."

"No, I haven't," replied her husband. "Honest. Have I, Mildred?"

Mildred shook her head.

"But, Mildred," said Mr. Haddock, "papa was going to give you just the biggest dinner ever."

Mildred looked very disconsolate.

"Well, bring the soup, anyway," said Mr. Haddock, "and we'll see."

The waiter bowed, said, "Very good," and left. His place was instantly taken by another, who handed Mr. Haddock a thin book. It was a list of wines.

[80]

"Ah!" said Mr. Haddock, rubbing his hands together. "Now you're talking," and to Mildred he said, "Ask him what is the name of the very best wine."

"Will," interrupted Mrs. Haddock, "I think I'd rather have just some water."

"Oh now, Hattie," said Mr. Haddock, "please. You can get water anywhere."

"Water quenches the thirst every bit as well as wine," replied Mrs. Haddock, "and it's much better for you."

"But it says in the Bible," said Mr. Haddock, "don't you remember—'Drink a little wine for your stomach's sake'? Doesn't it?" and he looked up appealingly at the waiter.

"Yes, sir," replied the waiter. "John XIV, 26. Would you like me to get you a Bible?" he added.

"I don't want wine," insisted Mrs. Haddock, firmly.

"Harriet," said Mr. Haddock, "would you doubt the Holy Writ? Would you sit here in front of our little daughter and suggest that perhaps not every word in that great Book is true? Would you have our Mildred's mind filled with doubt? You will be saying next," he added triumphantly, "that men come from monkeys."

"Château Yquem," suggested the waiter, "is a very good white wine," and he pointed to the last name on the card under the heading of "Bordeaux."

Mr. Haddock looked at Mrs. Haddock with a pleading smile, and then the smile slowly died on his face.

"I think," he said to the waiter, "that we'll just have some water."

"Yes, sir," said the waiter, and he sadly took the card and turned to go.

Mr. Haddock called him back. "Mind you," he said, "the very best water to be had."

"Yes, sir," replied the waiter, and withdrew.

"And now," said Mr. Haddock once more cheerfully, "that settles that. What do you think we'd better have next?"

"I don't know," said Mrs. Haddock, gloomily.

The waiter returned with the soup.

"What would you recommend to follow this?" Mr. Haddock asked him.

"A filet of sole is very good," said the waiter, "and then I would recommend the roast duck *à l'orange.*"

"How does that sound, Hattie?" asked Mr. Haddock.

Mrs. Haddock looked at the menu. "I think," she said, "I would like some spinach and some boiled rice."

"But, Hattie," objected Mr. Haddock, "you aren't going to be a vegetarian in Paris, are you?"

Mrs. Haddock shook her head resolutely in the affirmative. "It said in that article," she said, "to be especially careful during the summer months."

There was a moment of silence.

"Then I'll take the roast duck," said little Mildred, unexpectedly.

Mr. Haddock's face quickly lighted up. "Good!" he cried. "That's more like it."

"And perhaps the filet of sole first," suggested the waiter.

Mr. and Mrs. Haddock

Mr. Haddock eagerly looked at his daughter.

"All right," she agreed, after a moment's hesitation.

"Fine!" said Mr. Haddock. "Two fish and two ducks and then some spinach and boiled rice for Mrs. Haddock—Mrs. William Haddock," he added.

"Yes, sir," said the waiter, writing it down.

"Now," said Mr. Haddock, rubbing his hands together, "for the soup."

After they had finished the soup, there seemed to be a bit of a wait, so Mr. Haddock sipped his water and looked around at the other tables in the restaurant.

"It's sort of nice and quiet," he said, "and French. And the objection to Americans," he added, "doesn't seem to apply to head waiters and cloak-room girls."

Just then, from the entrance outside, came the sound of a great deal of women's noisy laughter, and in the doorway appeared a party of five or six people in evening clothes.

"Ah!" said Mr. Haddock. "Fellow countrymen. How nice!"

The head waiter ushered the party to the table next to that at which the Haddocks were seated, and with a great deal of noise and cries of, "Oh, no, Fred, you come on over and sit beside *me*," and, "Where's the waiter? We want some cocktails right away," they took their seats.

"Will," said Mrs. Haddock, "those people have been drinking."

"Drinking!" said little Mildred. "They're cock-eyed!"

"Waiter," called one of the new arrivals. *"Waiter!"* he called louder.

"Yes, sir."

"Waiter, we want some more cocktails. How about you, Nellie?"

"A Bronx," replied Nellie, "and a double Martini for Mrs. Cushing."

"Four Bronxes," said the man, "and two double Martinis; and hurry up."

"Yes, sir," said the waiter.

"Say," called one of the men across the

table, "did you hear the one Bob pulled when we came in?"

"No!" they cried.

"Well, when we were getting out of the taxi-cab, some old French woman came up and tried to sell Bob some roses and all the French Bob knows is *'Voulez vous coucher avec moi,'* and so he says that to her and she gets sore as a crab and starts bawling him out."

"What did Bob do?"

"Oh—Bob just laughs at her and then gives her fifty francs."

"Did she take it?"

This question was greeted by a loud laugh and cries of: "Can you tie that!" "Did she take it!"

"Bob must be quite a joker," observed Mr. Haddock.

The Haddocks' fish and their neighbors' cocktails arrived simultaneously.

"Gosh!" said Mr. Haddock. "I wish you would take some of this, Hattie. It's awful good."

"No," said Mrs. Haddock, "but I'd like some bread and butter."

So, after a few minutes, an order of butter was served.

"I wonder," said Mrs. Haddock, "if we could get some bread like we have at home?"

"What's the French," asked Mr. Haddock of Mildred, "for 'bread like we have at home'?"

The waiter was questioned and shook his head, and then called the head waiter, but with no better result, and Mrs. Haddock in Paris was reluctantly forced to spread her butter on what is known in America as "French bread."

"I'm afraid you're not enjoying this very much, Hattie," said Mr. Haddock.

"Oh yes, I am," she replied, "only I wish those people at the next table wouldn't talk so loud. Everybody's looking at them."

"Well, anyway," said Mr. Haddock, "here comes your spinach and your rice."

But he was wrong. It was only the spinach.

"And the rice?" he asked the waiter.

"Do you want them both at once?" was the reply.

"Certainly," said Mr. Haddock.

So, after a consultation of three waiters and the head waiter, it was decided by a vote of three to one that the request of the American lady to have two vegetables served simultaneously should be granted, provided that the payments of interest on the French debt to America should be suspended until 1975. This Mr. Haddock willingly agreed to, provided that he be allowed to have two lumps of ice in his water.

For a moment it looked as though the conference were going to break up in a deadlock, but little Mildred saved the day by suggesting that Mr. Haddock content himself with one lump of ice until he could have an opportunity to be shown over the French battlefields and see just what damage the Germans had done. Mr. Haddock agreed, and both parties expressed themselves as very well pleased with the result of the conference, which seemed to promise a new era of international relations.

"And the duck is very nice, too," remarked

Mr. Haddock, with a smile. "Isn't it, Mildred?"

"Fine," replied she.

"Then why don't you eat it?" asked her father.

"I am," said the little girl.

"Mildred," said her mother, "is there anything wrong?"

"No, mother," replied Mildred. "I'm having a fine time. Everything's great."

The duck, the spinach, and the rice were duly eaten.

"Now," said Mr. Haddock, "for a wonderful dessert."

Mildred suddenly turned quite white and asked if she might be excused.

"Do you want me to come with you?" asked her mother.

"No, thank you, mother," said the little girl, and she got up and left in the general direction of a door.

"I'm worried about her," said Mr. Haddock, putting down the menu card.

"Why?" asked Mrs. Haddock. "Did she do anything this afternoon?"

"No—but she's been so *nice* the last hour or so," he replied. "Did you hear her say 'Will you *please* pass the salt, *mother dear*'? She hasn't said anything like that," went on Mr. Haddock, "since the summer of 1921, or was it the spring?"

"It was the spring," said Mrs. Haddock, "because it was the same month the City Hall burned down."

"Gosh!" said Mr. Haddock, "it would be too bad ——"

"I'm going to see," said Mrs. Haddock, and she got up. "Watch out for my purse, Will," she said.

"All right, dear," said Mr. Haddock, and he sat there gazing after his wife as she disappeared through the door.

"The little girl's quite sick," said the woman in charge of the ladies' washroom as Mrs. Haddock anxiously came in, and she pointed to a door behind which could be heard various distressing noises.

"What is it, dear?" asked Mrs. Haddock in a momentary lull.

Mildred shook her head. "Nothing," she said.

"Did your father give you anything to eat this afternoon?"

"No, mother," replied Mildred, "and don't tell him I'm sick now."

"Why not?" asked Mrs. Haddock.

"Oh, because," said little Mildred.

"Because why?" asked her mother. "Mildred, are you keeping anything from me?"

"I'm not keeping anything from anybody," said little Mildred, and she suited the action to the word. "Judas! I'm sick!"

"Is that all?" said her mother.

"I hope so," said the little girl, weakly.

Mrs. Haddock picked Mildred up and carried her tenderly over to a lounge.

"I'll be all right in a little while," said she. "You go on out and talk to father."

"We're going home," said Mrs. Haddock. "Immediately!"

"Oh, don't do that!" said little Mildred. "Please, don't do that."

"Why not?" asked her mother.

"Oh, because," said Mildred. "Don't you see? Father wants to give us a swell time and you eat spinach and rice and won't drink wine, and I tried to eat the damn fish and the duck and everything, and now I go and get sick on him." And tears came into the little girls eyes.

Mrs. Haddock wiped the perspiration off her daughter's forehead. "You wait here," she said, "and I'll be right back."

"Don't tell him. Please," said little Mildred.

Mrs. Haddock found Mr. Haddock gloomily staring into space, but when he saw her he smiled and began eating again.

"How is she?" he said.

"Will," said Mrs. Haddock, "I think we'd better go home."

"But I've ordered dessert," said Mr. Haddock.

"No," said Mrs. Haddock, "we'll have to

go. Mildred is really very sick at her stomach."

"Gosh!" said Mr. Haddock. "That's too bad," and he signaled for the waiter. "The check please," he said, "right away."

Another waiter appeared with a large bottle of champagne. "The gentlemen at the next table," he explained, "said you looked like an American, and they wanted you to have a drink on them."

Mr. Haddock looked across at the next table and smiled his thanks and then shook his head.

"Oh, come on!" they called. "You can't get that at home."

"I know it," said Mr. Haddock, "but we've got to go."

"Oh no, you don't," they cried. "This is Paris. Come on, join us."

But Mr. Haddock's check arrived. He joined his wife and daughter at the coat room and, with little Mildred between them, they went quickly out of the door and into a taxicab. And so ended Mr. Haddock's first dinner in Paris.

"I'm all right," Mildred kept insisting all the way home.

"Of course you are," said her father.

"I still don't see why," said Mrs. Haddock, "you ate that fish and that duck."

"Oh, shut up!" said little Mildred.

"Shut up, *mother dear*," corrected Mr. Haddock, "would be better."

Mildred tried to laugh.

"I only wish," said Mrs. Haddock, "that we didn't have that long ride in the elevator ahead of us."

"Oh, my God!" said Mildred, "you *would* have to mention that."

But within fifteen or twenty minutes they had arrived at the hotel, and soon little Mildred was safe in her mother's bed and her mother was sitting beside her holding one hand while with the other she from time to time stroked her daughter's forehead. Mr. Haddock stood at the foot of the bed and watched the two for some time, then went over to the window and looked out on the streets of Paris.

"It's an awful nice night," he said.

"Shhh!" said Mrs. Haddock. "I think she's going to sleep."

"I am like hell," said little Mildred, "with all those taxicabs going by."

"Hadn't I better go for a doctor, dear?" asked Mr. Haddock.

Mildred laughed. "That would be a good one," she said. "I'd like to see you. And besides, I don't feel so bad now, anyway."

Mrs. Haddock got up and turned out the last remaining light and they sat there for some time without saying a word. The noise from the street below grew gradually less until only an occasional honk was heard. Finally Mrs. Haddock came quietly over to her husband and whispered, "She's asleep."

"Good!" said Mr. Haddock, and they tip-toed into the other room.

"Isn't that just our luck?" said Mrs. Haddock, beginning to let down her hair.

"I don't really think she's so very sick," said Mr. Haddock.

"I don't know, Will," said Mrs. Haddock. "You never can tell."

Mr. Haddock did not reply, but walked nervously up and down the room several times and then stopped in front of the open window.

"It's an awful nice night," he said.

"You'd better start getting to bed," said Mrs. Haddock. "It's late, and if Mildred is better in the morning we've got a lot of sight-seeing to do."

Mr. Haddock looked at his watch. "It's only nine o'clock," he said, and he took a deep breath. "That seems awfully early to go to bed your first night in Paris."

Mrs. Haddock didn't reply, and finally Mr. Haddock walked over and picked up his hat.

"Where are you going?" asked Mrs. Haddock.

"Nowhere," replied Mr. Haddock. "I just sort of thought I'd like to take a little walk —get a bit of fresh air. Fresh air is wonderful for you."

Mrs. Haddock looked at her husband suspiciously.

"I'll be right back," said Mr. Haddock. He looked in at Mildred for a minute to see if she was asleep and then closed the door after him and went out.

When he reached the street, he stood for a minute and took several long, deep breaths and said, "Gosh!" Then he started in the direction of the Seine.

The river was very beautiful in the moonlight and Mr. Haddock walked a part of the way across the bridge and stood there, lost in thought.

The red lights from the bridges in both directions formed beautiful patterns with their reflections in the water, and the white lights along the bank on either side made Mr. Haddock think of the lights along Third Street back home. But it wasn't like Third Street, either. There was something personal about the river with its red and white lights and its many bridges, perhaps because it wasn't a very large river—not nearly as wide as Mr. Haddock had expected. And there was a reflection of the moon also, and because it was in the Seine the moon somehow became personal, too, and Mr. Haddock would have liked to talk to it.

Mr. Haddock wanted very much to talk to some one, but everybody that went past seemed very foreign and very forbidding, and that left only the moon. And then there arose the problem as to whether or not the moon spoke only French. This language business was getting to be a terrible bore. Here Mr. Haddock wanted to talk to the moon, and he didn't dare start for fear that the moon would only look at him as so many people had that day, and then say something quite unintelligible, and expect Mr. Haddock to answer.

He took his small French conversation book out of his pocket and began looking for the section entitled: "With the Moon." He didn't find it, and he was just on the point of turning and going back to the hotel when he observed that another man was standing some distance farther on the bridge and, as Mr. Haddock watched, the man slowly began to climb over the railing, and it suddenly occurred to Mr. Haddock that he was probably going to throw himself into the water. So he ran up and caught hold of the man's coat just as he was preparing to jump.

"Listen," cried Mr. Haddock, but the man did not pay any attention and only stood there, gazing at the black water underneath. "Listen," said Mr. Haddock again. "Hey!"

The man slowly turned and looked at Mr. Haddock, who suddenly felt a little embarrassed.

"I just happened to be standing there," he said. "I wouldn't have bothered you, only— only I just happened to be standing there and I saw you climb over the railing and I said to myself, 'I bet that man is going to try to commit suicide,' and so I ran up and caught hold of your coat. And I hope you didn't mind," he added.

"Why did you stop me?" said the stranger, with a foreign accent.

Mr. Haddock shook his head. "I don't know," he said. "I guess it was because I wanted somebody to talk to. Are you an American?"

The man shook his head. "Russian," he replied, and he began again his preparations for jumping.

Mr. Haddock once more took hold of the man's coat. "Oh, now, look!" he said. "What do you want to do that for?"

"Because," replied the Russian, "there is no God."

"Why, there is, too," said Mr. Haddock.

"There isn't," said the Russian.

"Is," said Mr. Haddock.

The Russian tried to jerk away, but Mr. Haddock held on tightly.

"How do you know there is?" asked the Russian.

"Why, you can ask anybody!" said Mr. Haddock. "Ask a policeman," and he looked around for a *gendarme*. "There's one!" he cried. "Now you wait," and he let go the Russian's coat and ran to meet the French policeman who was walking slowly over the bridge.

"*Isn't* there a God?" cried Mr. Haddock, running up.

"Yes," replied the *gendarme.* "Law of August 5, 1798—Code Civil of Napoleon," he added.

"There!" said Mr. Haddock. "I knew there was." And taking the policeman by the arm, he rushed back to where the Russian had been standing. But the Russian, in the meantime, had jumped into the river, and Mr. Haddock, leaning over the railing as far as he could, was only able to distinguish the man's head as he came up for the first time.

"He says there is!" he shouted.

The Russian looked up.

"Who says there is?" he asked.

"Napoleon," replied Mr. Haddock.

The Russian smiled and sank quickly again.

"I think we'd better get him out," said Mr. Haddock, turning excitedly to the *gendarme.* "He might drown himself in that water."

"What is your name, please?" asked the *gendarme,* taking out a notebook.

"Haddock," said Mr. Haddock. "But let's save that man down there."

"Haddock?" said the policeman, writing it down. "And what is your prename?"

"But, listen," said Mr. Haddock, "that man's going to drown."

The *gendarme* peered over the railing. "May I see your passport, Mr. Haddock?" he said.

Mr. Haddock, instead of replying to this, suddenly pushed the *gendarme* to one side and was about to jump from the bridge toward the would-be suicide. At that moment, however, a small search-light appeared on the water, a rowboat filled with policemen shot out from under the bridge, and the Russian, dripping and exhausted, was hauled into the boat and rowed toward the shore, and that was the last Mr. Haddock ever saw of him.

"Well," he said, turning to the *gendarme,* "that was an interesting experience."

"Your passport, if you please," said the other, so Mr. Haddock showed his passport to the *gendarme.*

"That's my wife and little daughter," he said, pointing to the picture. "She's only ten,

[102]

but she's in the fifth grade already. You ought to hear her talk French, too."

The *gendarme,* however, did not seem to wish to hear any more about Mr. Haddock's family. He made a few notes, handed back the passport, and so, after one or two further but unrequited attempts at conversation, Mr. Haddock said good night and walked slowly along the bridge and back to the hotel.

Mrs. Haddock was waiting for him in the room.

"How's Mildred?" asked Mr. Haddock.

"Restless," replied his wife, "and feverish. And where have you been all this time?"

"Just walking around," said Mr. Haddock. "It's a beautiful night." And he began to undress.

"Say, Hattie," he said, as he was unbuttoning his shirt, "I met a very interesting Russian just now. He doesn't believe in God."

"Fiddlesticks!" said Mrs. Haddock. "Don't forget to lock the door," she added.

Just before getting into bed he peeped cautiously into his daughter's room. Little Mildred was lying with her arm behind her head and her eyes closed. Her father shut the door again softly, looked once more out of the window at the streets of Paris, and crawled into bed beside his wife, who was fast asleep. Mr. Haddock lay for some time thinking about the Russian, and then about little Mildred, and then about Mrs. Haddock.

"We'll have a better time to-morrow," he murmured, and finally he went to sleep.

CHAPTER V

H E was awakened by his wife, who was standing over him and shaking his arm. "Will," she said, "you'll have to get up." It was still dark outside. Mr. Haddock rubbed his eyes, blinked at the electric light, and then said: "What is it, Hattie?"

"Mildred," replied Mrs. Haddock. "She's worse. You'll have to go for the doctor."

Mr. Haddock jumped out of bed and started to dress. When he had finished, he looked in at his wife and daughter for a minute with a cheery smile, and then started on his way.

That was at 4:17 in the morning. At 8:40 on the same morning, reports began coming in to the police headquarters of the Fifth, Sixth, and Thirteenth Arrondissements that a demented American had been running around the streets frightening children and trying to break into houses. In several cases the reports came that he had thrown stones through upstairs windows of private homes and in one or two streets he had been seen to light bonfires in what seemed to be an attempt to attract attention. Finally a telephone message came that the madman was now sitting on the steps of the Pantheon.

And the report turned out to be true, for when a squadron of *gendarmes,* dispatched in haste from the nearest *mairie,* arrived on the scene, they found Mr. Haddock seated as described, in shirt sleeves and suspenders, and muttering gibberishly to himself.

In reply to the *gendarme's* question in French, Mr. Haddock only looked up, and then began again his wild, unintelligible croon. Finally, however, an interpreter was called and he was able, after some difficulty, to report that the gentleman was repeating a phrase which sounded to the interpreter like, "The lousiest city in the world—the lousiest people in the world—the lousiest buildings and trees

IN ONE OR TWO STREETS HE HAD BEEN SEEN TO LIGHT BONFIRES

and taxicabs and street cars and art galleries and churches and religion—"

The interpreter shook Mr. Haddock by the shoulder. "What are you doing here," he asked, "on the steps of the Pantheon, which contains, as you know, the tombs of several of our most distinguished citizens, such as, for example, Jean Jacques Rousseau, Voltaire, and Victor Hugo?"

Mr. Haddock stopped his muttering and replied, "I'm looking for a doctor."

This was translated to the *gendarmes* and was received with exclamations of astonishment and cries of, *"Alors,"* and *"Par example."*

The interpreter once more addressed Mr. Haddock. "But, my dear man," he said, "there are no doctors in Paris in July."

"Don't I know it!" groaned Mr. Haddock.

"And if there were," said the man, "you couldn't see them until two in the afternoon."

"But my daughter's sick," said Mr. Haddock.

The interpreter translated this last fact to

the *gendarmes,* who received it with sympathetic gestures and cries of, *"Alors,"* and *"Par exemple."*

Then, after a brief consultation, it was evidently decided that nothing was to be done to the *pauvre* American *père* whose *fille* was *malade,* and they all marched away, leaving Mr. Haddock more alone than ever on the steps of the Pantheon, which is situated on the Mont de Paris, the highest point on the left bank (two hundred feet) and the burial place of Ste.-Genevieve, patron saint of Paris (422-509 or 512 A. D.).

Mr. Haddock finally arose, brushed off his trousers, adjusted his tie, and got dejectedly into a taxicab.

"The Hôtel de New York and Sainte-Agnes," he said, "and go to hell." And after that Mr. Haddock felt a little better.

He felt much better when he arrived at the hotel and found that Mrs. Haddock had in some way been able to get hold of an American doctor and that Mildred was only a little "knocked out" by the change in food and climate and that she would probably be all right in a day or two.

After the doctor had gone, Mr. and Mrs. Haddock went into consultation in the next room.

"Well," said Mr. Haddock, "it's just one of those things that happen."

"And in the meantime," said his wife, "I'm going to stay right here and look after her."

"We can take turns," said Mr. Haddock. "Or we might get a nurse."

"We'll do nothing of the kind," said Mrs. Haddock. "Before I'd trust one of those French nurses—"

Mr. Haddock yawned.

"Well," he said, "it looks as though you and Mildred were certainly going to enjoy Paris."

He yawned again. "I'm a little sleepy," he said. "I think if you don't mind I'll lie down a bit," and he began lowering the shades.

Mrs. Haddock went into Mildred's room and Mr. Haddock closed his eyes and almost instantly went to sleep.

When he woke up again he had a great deal

of difficulty remembering where he was. He had been dreaming about the lumber business back home and this room didn't look like the lumber business back home. Then it suddenly dawned on him that he was in Paris and it struck him like a flash that he shouldn't be lying there sleeping when he could be out seeing French life, and then he remembered Mildred and Mrs. Haddock and he slowly got up and looked at his watch. It was two o'clock.

"Well, anyway," he said, "I've seen the Pantheon."

Mrs. Haddock tiptoed into the room, and in response to Mr. Haddock's anxious look she put her finger to her lips and said, "Asleep."

Mr. Haddock felt relieved. "Had any lunch?" he whispered.

She shook her head.

"I'll go out and get you some sandwiches," said Mr. Haddock, "and then I'll go over and see if we have any mail."

When Mr. Haddock left the hotel ten minutes later, it seemed to him that the best place to go for sandwiches would be a dairy lunch,

[110]

and when Mr. Haddock had been half an hour looking for a dairy lunch, it seemed to him that if he wasn't careful he would end up once more on the steps of the Pantheon. So the next restaurant he came to happened to be called *"La Pelouse"* and Mr. Haddock entered and was shown immediately upstairs by an extremely polite head waiter.

"Madame is waiting," he said.

"But I only want some sandwiches," said Mr. Haddock.

The waiter smiled and opened the door of a private dining room and motioned Mr. Haddock to enter. There in a small room was a table set for two, and at one side of the table sat what seemed to Mr. Haddock to be the most beautiful Frenchwoman he had ever seen.

"A ham sandwich," said Mr. Haddock to the waiter, "and a cheese sandwich."

The lady smiled and held out her hand to him.

"And no mustard on the ham sandwich," said Mr. Haddock, taking the lady's hand and pressing it to his lips as he had seen some-

[111]

body or other do in a moving picture at the Bijou, or maybe it was the Star.

"I'd sort of hoped women would be like this," said Mr. Haddock, "in Paris."

"Paris," murmured the lady, "never disappoints."

"That's true," said Mr. Haddock. "That's very, very true."

There was a moment of silence while the waiter disappeared.

"Tell me about Paris," said Mr. Haddock, sitting down.

"Have you seen the Eiffel Tower?" asked the lady.

"Yes," said Mr. Haddock.

"Have you seen the Arc de Triomphe?"

"Yes," replied Mr. Haddock, moving a little closer.

"Have you seen ——"

"What is this?" asked Mr. Haddock. "A game?"

"Have you seen Napoleon's tomb?" asked the lady.

Mr. Haddock shook his head.

"Let me tell you about Napoleon's tomb," said the lady.

"All right," said Mr. Haddock.

"Napoleon's tomb," began the lady, "thirteen by six and a half feet and fifteen feet high, is of antique red granite from Finland and was presented by Czar Nicholas the First."

"Indeed!" said Mr. Haddock.

"It rests on a pedestal of green granite," she continued, "and is surrounded by a gallery with ten bas-reliefs."

"Ten," said Mr. Haddock. "Well, well!"

"Facing the sarcophagus," she went on, after a minute or so, "are twelve colossal figures ——"

There was a knock on the door and Mr. Haddock leaped back to his chair. It was the waiter with two cocktails.

"Don't forget," said Mr. Haddock to the lady, "where we were."

The cocktails were duly served. Mr. Haddock gallantly raised his to the lady and made a bow.

[113] ·

"I give you," he said, "Napoleon's tomb."

"*À la vôtre,*" she replied, and smiled.

They drank and the waiter retired.

"And then," said the lady, "there's the obelisk."

"Isn't there, though," said Mr. Haddock. "I wonder," he added, making sure that the door was closed, "if you could tell me something about the Louvre, too."

"Ah," said the lady, "that would take all afternoon."

"Good!" said Mr. Haddock.

So the lady began.

"The Louvre," she said, "situated between the Rue de Rivoli on the north and the Seine on the south, is the most important public building in Paris——"

About four thirty another knock came on the door. "Who is it?" called the lady, after a minute.

"The gentleman's sandwiches are ready," said the waiter, outside.

"Ah yes," said Mr. Haddock. "Those sandwiches," and he prepared to leave.

[114]

"To-morrow," said the lady, "we'll take up the Latin Quarter, the Jardin des Plantes, and the Faubourg St.-Germain."

"My name is Haddock," said Mr. Haddock.

"I'm Mrs. Abercrombie," said the lady.

"How nice!" said Mr. Haddock. "Only, it doesn't sound very French."

The lady laughed. "I'm from Pittsburgh," she said.

"P-A?" said Mr. Haddock.

"P-A," replied the lady.

"Then you aren't French?" said Mr. Haddock, trying to keep the disappointment out of his voice.

The lady shook her head.

"Not even on your mother's side?"

The reply was negative.

"And Mr. Abercrombie?" asked Mr. Haddock.

"Mr. Abercrombie is in Pittsburgh," said the lady.

Mr. Haddock bit his lip.

"A wonderful city," he said, "and practically the center of the iron and steel industry of the whole world."

The lady laughed. "Don't forget," she said, "the Ritz bar at four, and do bring Mrs. Haddock."

"At least one of us will be there," said Mr. Haddock.

"How will I know Mrs. Haddock?" asked the lady, "if she comes alone?"

"You'll know her," said Mr. Haddock.

The lady held out her hand. *"Au revoir,"* she said.

Mr. Haddock once more kissed her hand, took his sandwiches, bowed, and went out.

On the narrow stairs he passed the head waiter, who was coming up, followed this time by two American gentlemen. Mr. Haddock smiled.

"These tourists," he remarked.

When he got outside, Mr. Haddock began to walk along the street, a trifle dejected, and after a little while he suddenly discovered that he was hungry. Mr. Haddock opened his bag and looked in.

"No," he said, "that wouldn't be right. Those belong to Hattie." And he continued on•his homeward way. "But," he added, as a sudden idea struck him, "I could always go back and get another sandwich." And he slowed down and stopped.

"No," he said, "that wouldn't be right, either. Mrs. Abercrombie or no Mrs. Abercrombie, I mustn't forget that I'm a married man with a family. Must I?"

But the gentleman who was passing did not answer.

"Must I?" called Mr. Haddock after him, but with no better result.

Mr. Haddock looked in the bag. There were still only two sandwiches.

"And if I eat one," he said, calculating rapidly, "that only leaves one."

He was standing, by that time, in front of a café, but, as far as Mr. Haddock could see, it was not a café where you could get anything to eat. On the window, however, was a sign in neatly raised white letters, *"Ici on Consulte le Bottin."*

[117]

Mr. Haddock read the sign over to himself. " '*Ici*' means 'Here,' " he said, "and '*Consulte*' certainly must mean 'Consult'—'Here consult—Le Bottin.' "

Mr. Haddock looked up. Coming out of the café was a middle-aged or bearded man in a blue uniform on whose hat was most distinctly "*Le Bottin.*"

Mr. Haddock smiled. "Are you the '*Le Bottin*'?" he asked.

The man nodded.

"Can I consult you?" asked Mr. Haddock.

The man nodded again.

"Well, look," said Mr. Haddock, "here my wife asked me to go out and get two sandwiches, and I've got the sandwiches; only, that was two hours ago, and now I'm hungry, but if I eat one of the sandwiches I'll have to go back and get another one and I really oughn't to go back to get another one."

"Yes," said the Bottin. "Why not?"

"Did you ever hear of a Mrs. Abercrombie," asked Mr. Haddock, "of Pittsburgh, Pa.?"

"Sit down," said the Bottin.

So he and Mr. Haddock sat down at one of the little round tables and the Bottin ordered a couple of drinks.

"Now," said he, "tell me that all again."

Mr. Haddock told him it all again and at the end the Bottin stroked his beard reflectively. Finally he spoke. "Let's see the sandwiches," he said.

Mr. Haddock pulled them out and to his great dismay discovered that they had put mustard on the ham sandwich.

"Darn these French!" said Mr. Haddock. "Mrs. Haddock doesn't like mustard. And I told them so."

"Yes," said the Bottin, "but that solves your problem," and breaking the sandwich in two, he gave half of it to Mr. Haddock and began to eat half himself.

Mr. Haddock was delighted.

"And these are awfully good, too," he said, tasting his drink. "What do you call it?"

"That's an Anis," said the Bottin.

"Is it really?" said Mr. Haddock. "It tastes a little like what we Americans used to

[119]

call absinthe. I got some in New Orleans
once."

"Absinthe," said the Bottin, "is forbidden
in Paris."

"Indeed!" said Mr. Haddock. "I didn't
think anything was forbidden in Paris."

He sipped the green cloudy liquid reflectively.

"Does this pay well?" he asked the other.

"What?"

"Being a Bottin," said Mr. Haddock.

The other shook his head sadly. "Nothing
pays well," he replied, "in France."

"That's too bad," said Mr. Haddock, and
then suddenly he was struck with a great idea.
He thought it over for several minutes, considered it from every angle, and then spoke.

"Look," he said, "do you want to make some
money?"

The Bottin shrugged his shoulders. "Will
I have to work?" he asked.

"No," said Mr. Haddock. "It's like this.
You're the Bottin, aren't you?" and he turned
around and pointed to the sign on the window.

The other nodded. "And people consult you, don't they, about everything?"

The Bottin did not reply.

"Well then," said Mr. Haddock, becoming more and more enthusiastic. "Here's my proposition. I and my wife and daughter are going to be here for four days. And we've got to see all of Paris in that time. Now ——"

"But ——" interrupted the Bottin.

"But nothing," said Mr. Haddock, masterfully. "Here's the big idea. I pay you a thousand francs ——"

"When?" asked the Bottin.

"Right now," said Mr. Haddock, and he took his money out of his pocket. "I pay you a thousand francs," he continued, "and you become our *Bottin,* and whenever we want to know what to see or where to go or how to get a doctor or a taxicab or a sandwich or anything, we consult you."

"Wait a minute," said the Bottin.

"I can't wait," replied Mr. Haddock. "It's such a swell idea. Look—here's my passport and everything—that will show you I'm all right. And here's a letter about me to the French Chamber of Commerce from Mayor Albery. See? Can you read English?"

The Bottin took the passport and examined it slowly. Then he looked at Mr. Haddock curiously for a minute.

"By any chance—" he began, and then he stopped. "What was your wife's maiden name?" he asked.

"Quetch," replied Mr. Haddock. "Harriet Quetch, of near Cincinnati."

The Bottin stroked his beard.

"Then you accept?" asked Mr. Haddock. The Bottin nodded.

"Fine," cried Mr. Haddock, and he held out the thousand-franc note gleefully.

"No," said the Bottin, pushing the money away. "We'll try it at first without money and see how it goes."

"No, but listen," said Mr. Haddock, "I'm an American."

"That's all right," insisted the Bottin. "You keep your money for awhile."

Mr. Haddock slowly and incredulously put the note back in his purse.

"Shall we shake on it," asked the Bottin, "as you say in America?"

"Shake," said Mr. Haddock, "and let's have two more of these drinks."

"I tell you what I would advise first," said the Bottin.

"Atta boy!" said Mr. Haddock. "You tell me. That's what I'm paying you for."

"Well," said the Bottin, "I think we ought first of all to have something more in our stomach."

Both men looked at the bag.

"What would you suggest?" asked Mr. Haddock.

"A cheese sandwich, perhaps?" said the Bottin.

"Bottin," said Mr. Haddock, "you're a wonder." And so they slowly and contentedly ate the other sandwich.

"I feel a lot better," said Mr. Haddock, "and a lot steadier, and so I think I'd better go on home. And I think," he added, "that you had better come with me and sort of explain my delay, because I'm not very good at explaining."

"At your service," said the Bottin, and so they paid the bill and the two men got up and started off toward Mr. Haddock's hotel.

CHAPTER VI

ON the way home, the Bottin took Mr. Haddock into a pastry shop, where Mr. Haddock enthusiastically bought a great many articles for Mrs. Haddock's late lunch. A few minutes later, with both their arms full of packages, they stood outside the Haddocks' door and Mr. Haddock, after taking a deep breath, knocked.

There was a moment of suspense, and then Mrs. Haddock came to the door and opened it slowly and cautiously.

"Hello, dear!" said Mr. Haddock. "I'm a little late."

Mrs. Haddock did not reply.

"I have brought a friend," said Mr. Haddock. "A French gentleman."

"Will Haddock," said Mrs. Haddock, "you come in here."

"Yes, dear," said Mr. Haddock, and to the Bottin he whispered, "You wait right here and I'll explain everything."

The Bottin waited.

A few minutes later the door opened and Mr. Haddock's face appeared.

"Pst!" he said, and the Bottin came over to the door. "Perhaps it would be better," whispered Mr. Haddock, "if you came in some other time. Mrs. Haddock is thinking of lying down."

The Bottin smiled and winked and began handing his share of the groceries over to Mr. Haddock.

"I'll see you to-night," whispered Mr. Haddock. "Come on around after dinner."

"At your service," said the Bottin, and he touched his cap and disappeared.

"Here's the rest of your lunch, dear," said Mr. Haddock, slamming the door shut with his foot.

"Has that man gone?" asked Mrs. Haddock.

"Yes, dear," said Mr. Haddock.

They were interrupted by a call from the other room.

"Father," cried little Mildred.

"Coming, dear," said Mr. Haddock.

"You waked her up," said Mrs. Haddock.

Mr. Haddock opened the door and looked in at his daughter. "Hello there!" he said.

"Hello!" replied the little girl, feebly. "What's mother crabbing you about?"

"She wasn't," said Mr. Haddock.

"I want a drink of water," said little Mildred.

"I'll get it, dear," said Mrs. Haddock, coming through the door.

"No," said little Mildred, "I want father to get it."

So Mr. Haddock walked quietly over toward the water pitcher.

"Stop tiptoeing," said the little girl. "And, for God's sake, stop whispering."

Mr. Haddock held the glass to his daughter's lips and she looked up into his eyes.

"You've been drinking, haven't you?" she said.

"Only Anis," replied her father; "it's very mild."

Mildred finished her water, closed her eyes, and her father and mother left.

"I think she's getting better," said Mr. Haddock.

"The doctor was here again this afternoon," said Mrs. Haddock, "and he says that it's only a light case. Incidentally," she said, "he very kindly arranged about having Mildred's and my meals sent up from a restaurant near here."

Mr. Haddock looked very penitent. "I really would have come back sooner with those sandwiches," he said, "only I happened to run into the Bottin."

Mrs. Haddock surveyed the various cans and paper bags which Mr. Haddock had brought back with him.

"We can use these," she said, "for dinner."

"Now don't you bother about that," said Mr. Haddock. "I'll just run out after awhile and get a bite."

Mrs. Haddock looked at her husband. "You'll do nothing of the kind," she said.

"Oh, but shoot!" said Mr. Haddock. "I told the Bottin I'd go with him about eight."

"You're going to stay right here," said Mrs. Haddock, "all evening."

"Oh, please!" said Mr. Haddock.

"No!" replied Mrs. Haddock.

Mr. Haddock kicked the leg of the bed several times, then walked to the window and stood looking out with his hands disconsolately plunged into his pockets.

"You never let me go out," he said.

Mrs. Haddock did not reply, but began humming "The Swanee River" softly to herself as she commenced to prepare supper.

Suddenly Mr. Haddock noticed that he was being watched by a pair of eyes from behind a blind in a window of the hotel across the way, and then slowly the blind was pushed cautiously aside and Mr. Haddock found himself staring at what was probably the most beautiful Frenchwoman he had seen since four thirty that afternoon. She smiled, a French smile.

Mr. Haddock grinned and adjusted his necktie.

"Will," said Mrs. Haddock.

"What?" replied he.

"What are you doing?"

"Just looking out the window," he replied. "Gosh! it's going to be another wonderful night."

"Open this can," said Mrs. Haddock.

Mr. Haddock signaled to the lady that his wife, Mrs. Haddock, wanted him to open a can of something, probably sardines, and left the window.

"Oh," said Mrs. Haddock, when her husband had finished opening the can and part of one finger, "those aren't the kind I like."

"Then I'll go right out," said Mr. Haddock, "and change them," and he reached for his hat.

"Will Haddock!" said Mrs. Haddock, so Mr. Haddock put his hat down again and returned to the window.

The lady had disappeared, so Mr. Haddock began to whistle.

"You'll wake Mildred up," said Mrs. Haddock.

"Can't I do *anything?*" said Mr. Haddock.

"You can slice some of this bread," said Mrs. Haddock.

In ten or fifteen minutes dinner was ready, and by the time they had finished it had begun to get dark outside.

"Another swell night," observed Mr. Haddock.

Mrs. Haddock had taken out her guide book and begun to read.

"There's a beautiful description in here," she said, "of Napoleon's tomb."

Mr. Haddock glanced at her quickly and then out the window. There was a light behind the blinds across the way, a soft red light. Mr. Haddock yawned and passed his hand across his face.

"I think I'll shave," he said.

Mrs. Haddock looked up. "You'll what?"

"Shave," said Mr. Haddock, defiantly.

"What in Heaven's name for?" asked she.

"Because I need one," said Mr. Haddock.

"Doggone it, Hattie, a man ought to look as well in his own home as he does anywhere else.

"The trouble with American husbands," he added, "is that they don't pay enough attention to their wives."

Mrs. Haddock looked up in alarm. "Will Haddock," she said, "the sooner we get back home the better it will be. And you didn't get the mail this afternoon, did you?"

"We Anglo-Saxons," continued Mr. Haddock, "have the wrong idea about marriage. A man's wife should be more than a wife—she should be his mistress."

"Will Haddock!" said his wife, "you've gone crazy."

"Marriage," said Mr. Haddock, "is ——"

He was interrupted by a whistle from the street outside. This was followed by a call, "Oh, Mr. Haddock." Mr. Haddock ran to the window and looked out.

"It's the Bottin," he announced, "and he wants me to come on out."

"Well, tell him that you can't," said Mrs. Haddock.

"Why not?" asked Mr. Haddock.

"Because you can't," said Mrs. Haddock.

Mr. Haddock returned to the window and announced the sad tidings, and there was sience in the street below.

Mrs. Haddock returned to the perusal of her guidebook. Suddenly she looked up.

"What are you doing now?" she said.

"Nothing," said Mr. Haddock.

Mrs. Haddock glanced around the room and then went on reading. All at once she sniffed.

"Will," she said, "you are playing with matches."

Mr. Haddock blushed guiltily and hid something behind his back.

"No, I'm not," he said.

From behind the blind across the street came the sound of music and a woman's laugh.

"And what's more," said Mr. Haddock, "we Americans must come to understand that our standards of sex are not necessarily the only

[133]

standards. Why, when I think ——" he began.

He was interrupted by a knock. A gentleman in a silk hat and a beard was at the door.

"Telegram for Mr. Haddock," he said.

Mrs. Haddock regarded the man suspiciously while Mr. Haddock opened the message. It read: "Don't be surprised at anything that happens. Count on me," and it was signed, "Bottin."

"Any bad news, Will?" asked Mrs. Haddock, hopefully.

Mr. Haddock handed the message back to the bearded man.

"My good fellow," he said, "you must have made a mistake. This message isn't for me."

The man in the beard winked.

"Awfully sorry, sir," he said. "Isn't this Monday?"

"No," said Mr. Haddock. "Tuesday."

"Ah," said the man, "that explains it," and he bowed and left.

Mrs. Haddock looked up at Mr. Haddock. "I've seen that man before," she said.

"What! That fellow?" said Mr. Haddock, with a laugh. "A mere telegraph fellow. A coxcomb. Why girl, you're mad."

"Nevertheless," said Mrs. Haddock, "I've seen him before."

"Impossible!" said Mr. Haddock. "He's never had that hat on before. And besides," he added, "who are you, to go around saying that you've seen this or that person before, when you can't even speak the language?"

At that moment an arrow came through the window and stuck with a sharp thud in the door behind Mrs. Haddock's head.

"Will Haddock," said Mrs. Haddock, "where did that come from?"

"Where did what come from?" said Mr. Haddock.

"That arrow."

"Oh!" said Mr. Haddock. "*That* arrow!" And he walked over and pulled it out of the door. "Hmm," he said.

He went to the window and looked out.

"There's a message on it," called someone from below in a disguised voice.

"Who's that?" asked Mrs. Haddock of Mr. Haddock.

"Who's that?" called Mr. Haddock out of the window.

"Nobody," came the reply from below.

"Nobody," said Mr. Haddock.

"I thought I heard some one," said Mrs. Haddock.

"No," said Mr. Haddock. "It must have been something you ate."

Mrs. Haddock got up and came to the window. While she was peering out, Mr. Haddock took the message off the arrow and read. "Courage," it said, and was signed, "Bottin."

"I'm sure," said Mrs. Haddock, sniffing once more, "that I heard somebody."

"Well, to tell you the truth," said Mr. Haddock, "I've got a confession to make to you."

His tone was serious.

"Oh, dear!" said Mrs. Haddock. "Have you been making a fool of yourself with women again, Will?"

Mr. Haddock shook his head.

"No, dear," he said, "and I don't see how you can think that about me."

He was silent for a minute.

"This is something," he went on, "that I've been wanting to tell you all my life and never dared. Hattie," he said at last, "I'm a ventriloquist."

"You're a *what?*" said Mrs. Haddock.

"A ventriloquist," said Mr. Haddock.

"You're a fool!" said Mrs. Haddock.

"No, honest," said Mr. Haddock. "I can throw my voice. That was really me talking all the time to myself in the street down there."

Mrs. Haddock still looked doubtful.

"I'll believe it," she said, "when I hear it."

"All right," said Mr. Haddock. "I'll make believe I'm talking to a man outside the door— a Chinaman, just to make it harder—and I'll eat a banana while I'm doing it."

"There aren't any bananas," said Mrs. Haddock. "I tried to get some and the man had never heard of bananas."

"Well," said Mr. Haddock, "I'll eat a bunch of grapes."

He picked up the grapes and put several in his mouth.

"Would you like to blindfold me?" he said.

"No," said Mrs. Haddock. "I would like you to stop this foolishness, and for Heaven's sake sit down and read something."

Mr. Haddock, however, was insistent.

"Hello!" he called. "Hello, you Chinaman. What are you doing outside that door?"

There was a moment of silence, and then the reply came back in a very high voice, "Hello!"

Mr. Haddock looked in amazement at Mrs. Haddock.

"Did you hear something?" he said.

"Yes," she replied.

"So did I," said Mr. Haddock. "I wonder who it is."

"Hello!" called Mr. Haddock again. "Who are you?"

"Me a Chinaman," replied the voice.

"My gosh!" said Mr. Haddock.

Mrs. Haddock got up and opened the door quickly, and there stood a Chinaman, with a beard. In his hand he held a big round cake.

"Me bake cake," he explained. "Heap good cake," he added.

"How much?" asked Mrs. Haddock, suspiciously.

The Chinaman looked as though he did not understand.

"How muchee?" translated Mr. Haddock.

The Chinaman shook his head.

"Nothing," he replied. "It's a birthday cake. Velly old Amelican custom."

"But it isn't my birthday," began Mr. Haddock, and then he saw the Chinaman close one eye in a bland, Oriental wink, so he stepped forward and took the cake with a smile.

"Isn't that nice of him, dear," said Mr. Haddock to his wife.

The Chinaman bowed to Mrs. Haddock, turned, and noiselessly disappeared.

"Well, well," said Mr. Haddock, "this wouldn't happen to us back home."

"Will," said Mrs. Haddock, "I've seen that man somewhere before."

"Nonsense!" said Mr. Haddock. "He would have said something about it. People don't forget you, dear," and he bowed gallantly.

Mrs. Haddock took the cake over to a table, moved some of the unopened canned goods out of the way, and prepared to cut into it.

"It doesn't cut very easily," she said. "And I don't think that Chinamen have beards like that, either."

"I wish that Mildred could have just a bite," said Mr. Haddock. "She loves cake."

Mrs. Haddock stopped cutting and pulled something out of the inside.

"Well, well!" said Mr. Haddock. "A saw."

Mrs. Haddock reached within the frosting and extracted two more small, fine-toothed saws, then a bit of candle and some matches.

"Will," said Mrs. Haddock, "something's funny about this cake."

"I know it," said Mr. Haddock. "There ought to be a rope ladder somewhere. Look farther, dear."

But there wasn't any rope ladder. There was, however, a note which Mrs. Haddock opened and read.

"I thought so," she said, looking at Mr. Haddock. "A Chinaman, indeed!"

"What's it say, dear?" he asked.

"It says: 'It's always darkest just before dawn,' and it's signed," she added, " 'Bottin.' And what's more," she concluded, "you're not going out to-night."

Then suddenly she stopped and put her finger to her lips and said, "Shhh!"

"How can I 'Shhh,' " objected Mr. Haddock, "when it was you who was talking?"

"Shhh!" said Mrs. Haddock. "Listen."

Mr. Haddock listened.

There was a faint scratching noise in the ceiling at one corner of the room.

"Mice," said Mr. Haddock.

"Shhh!" said Mrs. Haddock.

"And I suppose," he went on, a little bitterly, "that if a mouse does appear, you'll think it's the Bottin and tell me you've seen that face somewhere before. You women are all alike," he added.

The scratching grew louder, and soon little bits of plaster began dropping down onto the floor. Then suddenly a whole hunk of the ceiling fell with a bang into the room.

"Damn it!" said a voice.

Then there was a moment's silence, after which came a cautious whisper, "Haddock."

Mrs. Haddock motioned to her husband not to reply.

"Hey, Haddock!" came the whisper, this time a little louder.

There was no answer, and then slowly a face appeared in the opening.

"I thought so," said Mrs. Haddock, and she stepped forward.

"Oh, hello!" said the Bottin. "I'm afraid I disturbed you."

Mrs. Haddock did not reply.

"Is Mr. Haddock here?" asked the Bottin.

"Yes," said Mrs. Haddock, "and he's going to stay here."

"Hello there!" said Mr. Haddock. "Where have you been all evening?"

"Mother," called little Mildred from the next room.

"There now, see," said Mrs. Haddock.

AND THEN SLOWLY A FACE APPEARED IN THE OPENING

"I'm sorry," said the Bottin.

Mrs. Haddock gave an angry glance at the two men and went to soothe her daughter.

"Any chance?" whispered the Bottin.

Mr. Haddock shook his head doubtfully.

"Father," came the cry.

"Coming, dear," called Mr. Haddock, and asking the Bottin to excuse him for a minute, he hurried into the next room.

"What is it, dear?" he asked.

"She wants to know," explained Mrs. Haddock, a little angrily, "who you're talking to."

So Mr. Haddock told little Mildred all about the Bottin—how he had met him that afternoon, how he had conceived the wonderful idea of getting the Bottin to help him while they were in Paris, and how Mildred's mother had objected to his plan.

"It sounds fine to me," said the little girl.

"There!" said Mr. Haddock, triumphantly, to his wife. "You see?"

"Tell him to come on down," said little Mildred. "I want to see what he looks like."

[143]

"Not to-night, dear," said Mrs. Haddock. "You're sick, you know."

"That's right," said her father.

"I don't care," said little Mildred. "I want to see him *now,* and I won't take any more medicine and I won't go to sleep, and that will bring on a fever and possibly other complications and I may be sick for weeks."

"Well," said Mr. Haddock, "that seems to settle *that.*"

And he went hastily into the other room and stood below the hole where the Bottin was peering through the ceiling.

"Are you doing anything special to-night?" asked Mr. Haddock.

"No," replied the Bottin.

"Would you mind, then," asked Mr. Haddock, "coming down for a little while? My daughter wants to see you."

"Why, certainly," replied the Bottin.

And in a few minutes he knocked at the door and was let in.

"This is my wife," said Mr. Haddock.

"I almost feel that I know you," said the Bottin, "I've heard so much about you."

"And this is my daughter," said Mr. Haddock. "She's sick."

The Bottin seemed a little embarrassed under Mildred's frank scrutiny.

"Would you like," he asked, "to hear my watch tick?"

Mildred laughed. "No," she said.

"Would you like," suggested the Bottin, "to ride a cock-horse to Banbury Cross?"

Mildred shook her head.

"Well," said the Bottin, "would you like to hear a story?"

"Do you know any good ones?" asked the little girl.

"Once upon a time," began the Bottin, "there was a princess and she was as good as she was beautiful. And she was married to a prince who was as handsome and brave as the day is long. And they were very, very happy."

"Would you mind," said little Mildred, "if I vomit?"

Mr. and Mrs. Haddock

"Not a bit," said the Bottin, cheerfully.

"Now," he continued, "would you like to hear any more stories?"

"I think," said little Mildred, "that that will be enough for to-night."

The Bottin said good night, as did also Mr. and Mrs. Haddock; they turned out the light, and the three withdrew.

"What will we do now?" said Mr. Haddock when they were once more in the other room.

"We'll stay right here," said Mrs. Haddock.

"Let's play games," said the Bottin.

"Kissing games?" said Mr. Haddock.

"No," said Mrs. Haddock. "Of course not."

"Let's play One Goal, Two Goal," said Mr. Haddock.

"All right," said the Bottin. "How do you play it?"

"I don't know," said Mr, Haddock. "But isn't it a swell name for a game?"

The three were silent for a few minutes. Finally the Bottin spoke.

"I tell you what," he said, "let's play Hide and Seek."

Mrs. Haddock looked around the room.

"There aren't any places to hide in," she objected, "and besides, you'll get everything all mussed up."

"No, we won't," said Mr. Haddock. "Come on, let's play that, anyway, and see how it goes."

"Who'll be It!" said Mrs. Haddock.

"You be It," said Mr. Haddock, "because you're the lady."

"All right," said Mrs. Haddock, and she closed her eyes and began to count.

"Five, ten, fifteen ——"

When Mrs. Haddock had reached five hundred she called, "All around goal are It," and opened her eyes.

And by that time Mr. Haddock and the Bottin had reached the street and were getting into a taxicab.

"She'll be awful sore," said the Bottin.

"It won't last," said Mr. Haddock. "She's

not the kind that stays sore. Where shall we
go?" he asked.

"Well," said the Bottin, "what would you
like to do?"

"I think," said Mr. Haddock, "that I would
like to have a glass of beer first. Let's go
somewhere close."

"All right," said the Bottin; he said something to the driver and in a few minutes they
were nearing a café situated across a square
from an old mediæval church.

Street cars were going by on one side, and
an auto bus swerved around the opposite corner, narrowly missing the Haddock taxicab as
it arrived at the curb.

"The Café des Deux Magots," read Mr.
Haddock, as they got out and sat down at a
table in the midst of the chattering crowd.
"Just the place."

"I think first," said Mr. Haddock, before
they had ordered, "that I had better telephone.
Hattie might worry."

"Have you ever tried telephoning in Paris?"
asked the Bottin.

"No," said Mr. Haddock, "but electricity is the same the world over."

"I'd better go with you," said the Bottin, and he spoke the truth.

After a brief twenty-five minutes, telephonic communication with Mr. Haddock's hotel was more or less established, and in another ten minutes Mr. Haddock was listening to his wife just as though she were in the next room. Fortunately, however, Mrs. Haddock wasn't in the next room, but Mr. Haddock promised to come home almost immediately.

When they once more reached the outside of the café, Mr. Haddock was dripping with perspiration and his beer tasted very good indeed. So he had another.

"Beer," said the Bottin, "never hurt anybody."

"The longer I'm with you," said Mr. Haddock, "the more pleased I am that I found you," and he ordered two more beers.

Mr. Haddock sat for several minutes after that without speaking. The moonlight on the age-worn tower of the church across the square made him think for a while of the moonlight on the First Presbyterian Church back home.

"It's sort of old, isn't it?" he said to the Bottin.

The Bottin nodded.

"St.-Germain-des-Prés," he said. Then he added: "The oldest church in Paris. Sixth century, some of it."

Mr. Haddock whistled. "Gosh!" he said. "That's a long time ago."

"Fourteen hundred years," said the Bottin.

"It gives you a funny feeling," said Mr. Haddock. "Or maybe it doesn't affect you that way."

The Bottin shrugged his shoulders.

"Have you ever been to America?" asked Mr. Haddock.

The Bottin nodded.

"Where?"

"Oh, different places," he replied. "New York—Middle West—California."

"New York," said Mr. Haddock. "What doing?"

"Studying," replied the Bottin. "And writing."

"Studying?" repeated Mr. Haddock. "Studying what?"

"America," was the reply.

"You won't find out much about America," said Mr. Haddock, "from living in New York."

"Yes and no," said the Bottin. "Let's have one more beer."

The drinks were brought.

"Well, what do you think about America?" asked Mr. Haddock.

"Is this an interview?" asked the Bottin.

Mr. Haddock grinned.

"No," he replied. "But I'm just curious."

"I'm writing a book," said the Bottin, "about what I think."

"Indeed!" said Mr. Haddock, interestedly. "And when will it be published. I'd like to get one with your autograph. I've got a daughter-in-law who collects autographed books."

The Bottin smiled and stroked his beard.

[151]

"Thanks," he said, "but it probably won't be published for a long time."

"And in the meanwhile ——?"

"And in the meanwhile," he continued, "I'm very happy to be what you call the Bottin."

"Yes, but you don't make much money," objected Mr. Haddock. "You told me so yourself."

The Bottin shrugged.

"I don't need much," he said, "and life here is very pleasant."

"Yes, but look, Bottin," said Mr. Haddock. "You're not getting ahead anywhere—I mean, what are you going to do when you get old?"

The Bottin smiled.

"That will take care of itself," he replied.

"But haven't you any ambition?" asked Mr. Haddock.

The Bottin nodded.

"You wouldn't understand it," he said. "It's sort of religious."

"I might," said Mr. Haddock.

The Bottin looked at him for a long time.

"TWO BEERS," SAID THE BOTTIN

"Yes," he said at last, "I think you might."

"You know, Bottin," said Mr. Haddock, "I sort of feel I can talk to you—I felt it right at once. It's because you're French, I guess. But, anyway, there's things I've wanted to talk over with people all my life, and I've been afraid. People, you know, Bottin, don't open up much, where I come from. You can't talk to them about things you really want to talk about. But over here in Paris—at this café anyway—sitting here with you it's all sort of different. Why, I feel I could ask you a thousand questions and you wouldn't think I was a damned fool, would you?"

"No," said the Bottin.

"Well, for instance," said Mr. Haddock, "all my life I've wondered whether the *Titanic* really sank to the *bottom* of the ocean, or whether it is still floating around halfway down, like it said in a Sunday newspaper article I read."

"That's something I don't know very much about," replied the Bottin.

"Neither do I," said Mr. Haddock, "and yet I've always felt that some day I'd meet somebody who could tell me. Now here's another thing," continued Mr. Haddock. "Tell me this: What's Art?"

"Art?"

"Yes," replied Mr. Haddock. "I mean, why should I go into the Louvre or some place and look at a lot of pictures or statues—or something?"

"Art ——" began the Bottin, and then he looked at Mr. Haddock and stopped.

"You see," said Mr. Haddock, a little sheepishly, "I'm so dumb—and I'm kind of ashamed to ask anybody. And so I've just gone along bluffing all my life. Why, my son or daughter would just laugh their heads off at me. And as for Hattie ——"

Mr. Haddock suddenly grabbed his watch from his pocket and looked at it.

"Oh my gosh!" he said. "I'd better be getting home."

"How about Hattie?" asked the Bottin.

"Well, she just doesn't sort of understand me at all," said Mr. Haddock. "But say, Bottin, there's a great woman—a great woman."

Mr. Haddock quickly finished his beer, shook hands, and prepared to go.

"I'll call around about nine in the morning," said the Bottin.

"You'd better telephone first," said Mr. Haddock, "just to be sure everything's all right."

"Good night, Haddock," said the Bottin.

"Good night, Bottin," said Mr. Haddock, "and thanks."

He walked slowly along the sidewalk in front of the many people seated there and then when he had come to the corner of another street, he turned for a minute and stood looking at the white crumbled beauty of St.-Germain-des-Prés. Then he went on.

Mrs. Haddock was asleep with the guidebook in her hand when he got back to the room, so he didn't bother to wake her up, and as quietly as possible he undressed, pulled on his pajamas, looked in for a minute at little Mildred, and went to bed.

"Gosh!" he said just as he was falling asleep. "Fourteen hundred years!" and that was all he remembered until the next morning.

CHAPTER VII

THE telephone had been ringing for some time when Mr. Haddock awoke. It was bright daylight, and Mrs. Haddock, fully dressed, was standing looking at the instrument.

"Answer it, Will," she said, "I'm afraid."

"Afraid of what?" asked Mr. Haddock.

"The French language. I answered it once yesterday."

Mr. Haddock took down the receiver, which was not at all like an American receiver, and said "Hello!"

It was the Bottin.

"Shall I come up?" he asked.

Mr. Haddock looked around at Mrs. Haddock and then said, "Call again in about half an hour," and hung up.

"I've arranged," he said to his wife, "for him to take you out this morning."

Mrs. Haddock shook her head. "I've got to stay here with Mildred," she said.

"How is she?" asked Mr. Haddock.

"Better," replied Mrs. Haddock.

"I can take care of her," said Mr. Haddock, "while you go out and see Paris."

Mrs. Haddock shook her head. "It wouldn't be right."

"Oh, doggone it, Hattie!" began Mr. Haddock, and then he said, "O.K., we'll both stay," and he went to the telephone to order breakfast.

"The usual breakfast," he said in reply to a question at the other end of the line. "You know—fruit, some kind of a cereal, oatmeal or something, and some scrambled eggs, and buttered toast, and coffee," and hung up the receiver.

Mrs. Haddock was laughing.

"Well," she said, "you'll get the coffee, anyway."

Mr. Haddock went in and said good morning to his daughter and returned when the breakfast arrived.

"What is this?" Mr. Haddock asked of the waiter.

"Coffee," replied the waiter.

Mr. Haddock tasted again.

"You may be right," he said. "You've lived here longer than I have. And what's that?"

"Milk," replied the waiter. "Hot milk."

Mr. Haddock poured the milk in the coffee, then looked up.

"An interesting experiment," he remarked, "proving that when you mix a dark, positive liquid with a light, negative liquid, the result is terrible. And if there's one thing I hate," said Mr. Haddock, "it's strings in my coffee."

"You can get them out, dear," said Mrs. Haddock, smiling triumphantly, "with a spoon."

"Of course I can," replied her husband, "but we're only going to be here such a short time."

And with that he took the *café au lait* and poured it quickly into the washbowl.

"There," he said, "that wasn't hard, was it? And besides," he added, "coffee is a drug and its constant use may lead to something worse. Although at the present time," he concluded, "I can't think of anything worse than what I just tasted. Now," he said, "for the rest of the breakfast."

The rest of the breakfast consisted of two rolls in the shape of a crescent.

"Delicious," murmured Mr. Haddock, "especially without butter."

The telephone rang again.

"Probably the French President," said Mrs. Haddock, "to apologize about there not being any butter."

But it wasn't the French President.

It was the Bottin again.

"What'll I tell him?" asked Mr. Haddock.

"Tell him no," she said.

So Mr. Haddock told the Bottin to call up again that afternoon.

"Now," said Mr. Haddock, "for another wonderful day in our hotel. And I wonder what we'll do," he added, "when we've finished reading all the guidebooks?"

"They're very interesting," said Mrs. Haddock, "and they make me want to see Paris very much."

"I saw a church last night," said Mr. Haddock, "that was built in the sixth century."

"What was the name of it?" asked Mrs. Haddock.

Mr. Haddock shook his head.

"I don't know," he said. "It was a French name. What difference does that make, anyway?"

"How are you going to tell anybody about it," said Mrs. Haddock, "if you don't know the name?"

"Why do I have to tell anybody about it?" asked Mr. Haddock.

"Sometimes, Will Haddock," said Mrs. Haddock, "you're a bigger fool than at others."

She picked up Mr. Haddock's breakfast tray and sat it outside the door in the hall.

"I could have done that," said Mr. Haddock.

"But you didn't," said his wife.

She brushed a few crumbs off the table into

the palm of her hand, looked around the room
for a waste basket, remembered again with a
frown that there wasn't any waste basket, and
took the crumbs to the window.

"Maybe there's some birds, Will," she said,
as she scattered the crumbs on the window
ledge. "I'd like to see some sparrows."

"There wouldn't be any birds in Paris,"
said Mr. Haddock.

"Why not?" asked his wife.

"I don't know," said Mr. Haddock. "It
just wouldn't seem right."

"Oh, look!" said Mrs. Haddock. "Come
here and look, Will! There's a man driving a
lot of goats through the street."

"See anybody we know?" asked Mr. Haddock.

He ran to the window and looked out. Sure
enough, passing below them was a Frenchman
in a black smock accompanied by a shepherd
dog, driving along a bevy, or perhaps a dozen,
black and white goats. Behind the man were
several taxicabs and an auto bus, honking
madly, but with no apparent effect on the un-

perturbed goatman, who, from time to time, put a small horn to his lips and blew a shrill blast.

"He's selling milk," said Mrs. Haddock. "Look."

Mr. Haddock ran in and picked little Mildred up out of her bed and carried her to the window. Finally the procession reached the corner of the street, the goats turned slowly to the right, and traffic was allowed to continue.

"I wish I had some goats like that," said little Mildred as her father put her back in bed.

"Father will get you some," said Mr. Haddock, "if you take your medicine and lie very quietly."

"Father," said little Mildred, "is just a cock-eyed liar."

But she took the medicine, nevertheless.

Mrs. Haddock glanced once more out of the window, then went over to her suitcase and took out some knitting.

"What are you going to do?" asked Mr. Haddock.

"Knit," she replied.

"How can you knit?" said Mr. Haddock. "There aren't any rocking chairs."

Nevertheless, Mrs. Haddock seated herself by the window and began. Mr. Haddock watched her for several minutes.

"What's that going to be?" he asked.

"A sweater," replied Mrs. Haddock.

"Who for?"

"Mrs. Patterson," replied Mrs. Haddock. "It's going to be a Christmas present."

"Which Christmas?" asked Mr. Haddock.

Mrs. Haddock did not reply.

"I should think you could do it faster," said Mr. Haddock, "if you used your right hand to go under and then pull it out with your left hand."

There was no answer to this except the slight clicking of the knitting needles.

"How many stitches do you take to a row?"

"Thirty-four," replied Mrs. Haddock.

"Why not thirty-six?" said Mr. Haddock.

"Will Haddock," said his wife, "you go in and talk to Mildred for a while."

So Mr. Haddock got up and went into Mildred's room.

In a few minutes there was a crash of falling glass.

"It's nothing, dear," called Mr. Haddock, quickly. "I was just doing a trick."

Mrs. Haddock sat down again and resumed her knitting. There came to her from the other room the sound of chuckles, then several "Shh's" and then Mildred burst into a loud laugh.

"Will," called Mrs. Haddock, "what are you doing?"

"Nothing, dear," said her husband.

Mrs. Haddock put down her knitting, got up, and went to the door.

Mr. Haddock, wearing one of his wife's hats, had taken off his shoes and was balancing himself in the manner of a tight-rope walker on the foot of Mildred's bed.

"Hello, dear!" he said, smiling somewhat foolishly. "Shall I come down?"

"That's my very best hat," said Mrs. Haddock.

"I know it," said Mr. Haddock. "The best is none too good for you," and he climbed off the bed.

Mrs. Haddock lowered the blinds until the room was almost completely dark, straightened up Mildred's bedclothes, put her hat away on the top shelf of the wardrobe, and went back to her knitting.

"Sit there," she said, pointing to a chair near the window, and Mr. Haddock sat down.

Suddenly a little bird flew up to the window ledge and began to eat the crumbs. Mr. Haddock watched it for a few minutes, then looked at Mrs. Haddock and slowly reached in his pocket for a piece of string. The bird flew away, and while it was gone Mr. Haddock made a noose and carefully placed it on the window ledge in the midst of the crumbs. Then, holding one end, he waited.

In a few seconds the bird came back, followed by two or three others, and with breathless interest Mr. Haddock watched it come nearer and nearer the center of his trap. Then suddenly, just as he was about to pull the

noose tight, he looked up and saw that the
French lady in the hotel across the way was
watching him and laughing. Mr. Haddock
blushed and smiled.

"Will," said Mrs. Haddock.

"Yes, dear," he replied, quickly putting the
string back in his pocket.

"If I let you go for the mail, will you come
right back?"

"Certainly," said Mr. Haddock.

Outside the hotel, Mr. Haddock hesitated
for a minute, debating with himself whether or
not to go up and say "Good morning" to that
nice French lady. But just at that second a
taxicab came along, so he decided to postpone
his visit, and in less than half an hour his cab
was pulling up outside the front entrance of
the American Express Company.

It was a very busy corner of old Paris, and
after Mr. Haddock had pushed his way
through three or four energetic newsboys who
wanted to sell him the New York and Chicago
papers, he found himself in a large room full
of healthy, well-dressed people, and for a sec-

ond Mr. Haddock thought he was back in Legion, Ohio, and it seemed very nice indeed.

He was directed in English toward an elevator in the rear, and in a few minutes he was upstairs, standing in line in front of a window marked "H to N."

"My!" said Mr. Haddock to the gentleman in back of him. "It seems good to see Americans again."

"I'll say it does," replied the gentleman. "This is the worst city in the world," he continued, "and the French, by God! are the most ignorant people I've ever seen. They don't know nothing."

"Indeed!" said Mr. Haddock.

"I tried for two hours this morning," said the man, "to get some Pluto water."

"That's an interesting criticism," said Mr. Haddock, "and if I were you I would write to your Congressman about it."

"Oh, I'm going to let them know about it, all right," said the man. "Wait till I get back home."

"I wouldn't wait that long," said Mr. Haddock. "Why don't you try some other kind of water?"

The man glanced suspiciously at Mr. Haddock and opened his mouth to reply.

He was interrupted, however, by the young man behind the mail counter telling Mr. Haddock he was next.

"Is there anything for Haddock?"

There was something for Haddock. Ten letters.

"Next," said the young man, and Mr. Haddock went happily over in the corner to open his mail.

Three of the ten letters were for Mrs. Haddock, one was for Mildred, and of the remaining, the first five contained blotters from the First, Second, Third, Fourth, and Fifth National Banks of Legion, Ohio.

"I'm glad I paid postage due on those," said Mr. Haddock, "because it's terribly difficult to get good bank blotters over here."

The tenth letter, however, was from Mr. Haddock's son, Frank, and Mr. Haddock himself was a little surprised to find how eager he was to read the news from home. There really wasn't much of importance, either, but it seemed very good to hear that the business was getting along very nicely, and that Ed Sanders had left Merkle & Company to go with Dobbs & Clawson, and that Pete Johnson had been elected to the Rotary Club.

Mr. Haddock put the letters into his pocket, pushed his way to the elevator, and descended to the first floor.

There seemed to be a great many women in the elevator and they all seemed to want to talk rather loudly about the French for such a small car, and Mr. Haddock was quite glad when he reached the first floor. And, besides that, he needed a shoe shine, so he walked up to the front office and down the stairs, where he found a very affable negro and a shoe-shining stand, and in a few minutes he had completely recovered his peace of mind.

"Don't any Americans who come to Paris," he asked the negro, "have a good time?"

The negro laughed.

"Ain't you having a good time?" he asked.

"Sure I am," said Mr. Haddock, "but all I've heard since I got in this building is a lot of complaints about the French."

"Race prejudice," said the negro, philosophically, "is a funny thing."

"Yes," agreed Mr. Haddock, "isn't it?" and he picked up a newspaper from the next chair and began to read.

"I see," he remarked, "that Americans stopping at the Hotel Continental in Vienna are Moe Rosenberg, Isadore Cohen, Franklin P. Ginsberg, and Mr. and Mrs. Otto Kalbfleisch."

The negro grinned but made no comment.

"Is this published here in Paris?" asked Mr. Haddock.

"Yes, sir," said the bootblack. "There's three American papers published here—two morning and one afternoon."

"Well, well!" said Mr. Haddock. "I must get them for my wife," and he read carefully through every column.

"The editorials," he remarked, "seem to be a little conservative—at least this one on 'The True Greatness of Shakespeare' does. And who, may I ask," he continued, "is Berry Wall?"

The negro laughed. "Don't you know Berry Wall?"

Mr. Haddock shook his head.

"Why," said the negro, "he's the leader of the American Colony here."

"The American Colony? Is there an American Colony in Paris?" asked Mr. Haddock.

The negro laughed long and loud.

"Is there!" he said. "Boy, you ought to see them!"

"I'd like to," said Mr. Haddock, "only I haven't seen Napoleon's tomb or Notre Dame yet."

"Neither have they," replied the negro.

He finished the shine with a snap and a flourish. Mr. Haddock paid and left.

On the way home Mr. Haddock decided to stop at the bank and get some more French money, because he discovered that in some way or other all the money he had conservatively set aside for Paris had been already spent and here it was only Wednesday noon. Mr. Had-

dock decided immediately to institute a strict
program of economy, and it seemed to him that
the best way to start the new régime would be
to give this taxi driver only a small tip. But
after they arrived at the bank and he had done
so, and the driver had looked at the tip and
then at Mr. Haddock, he decided that it
would perhaps be better to start economizing
along some other less personal line. So he
gave the man another franc, and as the driver
still refused to smile he gave him another.

"Hey!" said Mr. Haddock. "How much do
you want, anyway? Me not American—me
French. Honest I am," and Mr. Haddock
crossed his heart several times to convince the
man.

The driver shrugged his shoulders, put the
money in his pocket, and drove off. Mr. Haddock turned and walked into the bank.

It was an American bank and quite a bit
like the Second National at home, with the exception that the employees and the bankers
didn't seem to be in such a terrible hurry. In
fact, it was as though the air of Paris, seeping

in through the door, had affected the interior
of the bank in the same way that it had touched
and changed the exteriors of all those old buildings. And Mr. Haddock was beginning in
some way to understand how it was possible
for men in Paris—even bankers—to sit for an
hour or two at a café and watch people go by
when they really ought to be working.

It was as though, thought Mr. Haddock,
the French had learned to devote more time to
the problem of how to enjoy life instead of
consecrating all their energies to the intensive,
exhausting struggle which Mr. Haddock had
come to know as a young man when he first
went into "business." And in some way, which
Mr. Haddock could only vaguely sense, Paris
was beginning to affect him in the same way it
had apparently affected these nice-looking
young men who were so courteously leisurely
in cashing Mr. Haddock's letter of credit.

It was lunch time when he left the bank, so
he hurried home, and just before getting out
of his taxi Mr. Haddock remembered that it
might be a courteous thing to do if he were to

run up in the other hotel and just say "Hello" to that French lady across the way.

"But no," said Mr. Haddock, in the doorway. "That wouldn't be fair. I promised Hattie I would come right home. And besides," he added, "it's such a bright sunshiny day, and maybe she doesn't speak English, either."

So he went resolutely into his hotel and into his elevator and up to his room. And just as he was about to enter he heard Mrs. Haddock inside talking loudly to some one—some one who evidently was not Mildred.

"A Frenchman," flashed through Mr. Haddock's mind, and all the bad things he had heard about Frenchmen suddenly came to the surface. Perhaps one had gotten into their room—through the hot-water faucet or something.

"But that's just foolish," he said, and opened the door.

Mrs. Haddock was leaning out of the window, and as Mr. Haddock entered she was calling, "And I rinse them *thoroughly* in cold water afterward."

"Oh, Will," she said, turning, "I want you to meet Mrs. Ferguson."

Mr. Haddock advanced to the window.

The lady to whom Mrs. Haddock was talking was the French lady who lived in the hotel across the street.

"This is my husband," announced Mrs. Haddock.

Mr. Haddock bowed, a little dazed. The lady smiled and called, "Pleased to know you."

"But ——" said Mr. Haddock.

"Mrs. Ferguson's from Ohio, too," said Mrs. Haddock. "Cleveland. She was born in Akron, though."

"Oh yes," said Mr. Haddock.

"Mrs. Ferguson's husband couldn't come over to Paris," went on Mrs. Haddock. "Business," she explained.

"What a pity!" said Mr. Haddock. "I wonder if he knows a Mr. Abercrombie of Pittsburgh. They ought to get together, those two."

Mrs. Haddock continued the conversation with Mrs. Ferguson while Mr. Haddock went in and spoke to Mildred.

"Well, your mother seems to have found a friend," he said, "and your father is beginning to think that maybe Toledo, Ohio, would be a good place to hold the next French Revolution. And, Hattie," he called, "I don't really think that all the people on this quaint little street want to know the exact date I changed into my winter underwear last year, either."

Mrs. Haddock's reply was interrupted by the arrival of the waiter with the lunch.

"Oh yes," said Mr. Haddock, "and here's the mail—and a letter for Mildred from— from ——," and he tried to make out the postmark.

"That's all right where it's from," said little Mildred, snatching the letter greedily.

And Mrs. Haddock, too, was very excited about her mail, and it was some time before Mr. Haddock could induce them to taste any of the lunch.

[177]

It was quite a good lunch, too, and at the conclusion Mr. Haddock frankly said so.

"Yes," said Mrs. Haddock, "except that I don't trust these French sauces. Aunt Flora said that the French always use sauces to cover bad meat."

"But we had fish," objected Mr. Haddock.

"Bad fish," said Mrs. Haddock.

She picked up her letters and reread them for the fourth time.

"Will," she said at last.

"What, dear?" asked Mr. Haddock.

"Don't you suppose that we might sail a little earlier?"

"Why?"

"Oh, I don't know," said Mrs. Haddock.

"What's the matter?" asked Mr. Haddock.

Mrs. Haddock was silent.

Mr. Haddock got up and walked over to the window; then he came back and sat down.

"All right, dear," he said. "I'll see about it this afternoon."

"No," said Mrs. Haddock, "wait a couple of days, anyway. It's just that this hotel is sort of getting on my nerves. There's nobody to talk to and the servants don't understand anything I say and the man downstairs is very impertinent and says that we'll have to pay for that hole in the ceiling."

"That reminds me," said Mr. Haddock. "Has the Bottin called up?"

Mrs. Haddock shook her head.

"Somebody telephoned," she replied, "but when I answered, he didn't say anything, just hung up."

"That couldn't have been the Bottin," said Mr. Haddock. "He is very fond of you and always refers to you as 'that splendid woman.'"

Mrs. Haddock got up and began clearing away the dishes and Mr. Haddock lighted a cigar.

"Paris isn't so bad," he said, and he took Mrs. Haddock's hand and patted it. "You're just homesick," he said.

"No I'm not," said Mrs. Haddock. "I wanted to see Europe, and I'm going to see it."

[179]

"That's the spirit," said Mr. Haddock. "Well," he remarked, after a while, "if you don't mind, how would it be if I took a little walk?"

"All right," said Mrs. Haddock. "I'm going to lie down, anyway. I didn't sleep at all well last night, Will. I can't get used to these beds. And bring Mildred something to read when you come back."

CHAPTER VIII

MR. HADDOCK walked down the street past shops whose windows were full of paintings and engravings, past tobacco stores which he had learned to distinguish by a red diamond-shaped object suspended over the door, past windows full of images of saints and Sacred Hearts and Joan of Arc, past interesting gateways and glimpses of old courtyards within.

The people, too, attracted Mr. Haddock's attention—every one of them. They all seemed so different, so individual. School children in black smocks; nuns with large white caps and blue robes; priests in black cassocks and blacker beards; flower women, vegetable women, women street-car conductors with voices like claxon automobile horns; firemen in shiny brass helmets marching eight together like a squad of soldiers across the square.

The square itself happened to be the same one that he had visited the night before. There was the old Roman church and the Café des Deux Magots. And there was the Bottin.

"Hello!" said Mr. Haddock, happily.

The Bottin got up, lifted his hat, and motioned for Mr. Haddock to sit down.

"I called up," said the Bottin.

"Yes," said Mr. Haddock, "I know. My wife answered. What's that you're drinking?"

"A Vieux Marc," said the Bottin.

"Is it any good?" asked Mr. Haddock.

The Bottin looked hurt; in fact, for a minute Mr. Haddock thought he was going to cry.

"I'll take one," said Mr. Haddock, quickly.

"It's my favorite liqueur," said the Bottin, when Mr. Haddock's drink had arrived.

"Not bad," said Mr. Haddock, sipping. "I mean, it's wonderful," seeing the look which came into the Bottin's face.

"Wonderful," he repeated, smacking his lips.

"How is Mrs. Haddock getting along?" asked the Bottin after a few minutes, "and that nice little girl?"

Mr. Haddock shook his head gloomily.

"That's just what I want to see you about," he said.

"Good," said the Bottin.

After a few minutes Mr. Haddock began.

"You see, Bottin," he said, "I've sort of been looking forward to this trip for a long time, and not entirely," he added—"not entirely on account of myself.

"Mrs. Haddock," he went on, "needed a rest and a change. For twenty-five years she's been working; and Mrs. Haddock is the kind of a woman who isn't happy unless she's doing something useful—housework, the children, her club—you know."

"Yes," replied the Bottin, "the American wife."

"So," continued Mr. Haddock, "I thought that if we came over here she'd sort of take a vacation and play a bit, like she used to. Laugh and run around and forget her respon-

[183]

sibilities. I wanted her to have a good time every minute."

The Bottin nodded and sipped his liqueur.

"And, doggone it, Bottin," said Mr. Haddock, "so far, this trip's been just the doggondest flop ever! She's miserable—don't like the French—don't like the hotel—wants to go home—and at times I almost think she's afraid of enjoying herself. You know, Bottin, I'd be willing to bet she's really glad Mildred got sick just so that will give her something she can do.

"I wouldn't care so much," concluded Mr. Haddock, "only I'd sort of counted on it. When we first got married, we used to have a hell of a good time together, Bottin."

He was silent.

"Well," said the Bottin at last, "what'll we do about it?"

"Let's get a couple more of these drinks," said Mr. Haddock, "and then maybe we'll think of something."

"I'm awfully pleased," said the Bottin, "that you like that liqueur."

Several minutes passed in silent contemplation.

Their reverie was interrupted by an old woman standing on the sidewalk in front of them who suddenly, without any apparent reason, began to sing. Mr. Haddock listened for a few minutes and then turned to the Bottin for an explanation.

"It's her *métier*," replied the Bottin. "Her job. That's the way she earns her living."

The old woman finished her song and began passing the hat.

"What was she singing about?" asked Mr. Haddock. "Was it a hymn or something?"

"No," replied the Bottin, "it was about a woman who deceived her husband—made him *cocu*, you know. The second verse was really very witty."

"How did it go?" asked Mr. Haddock.

"Well," said the Bottin, "it would be hard to translate. French wit is different, anyway."

"Better?" challenged Mr. Haddock.

"Now don't go getting patriotic," said the

Bottin. "It's just different. Gallic. The French don't understand American humor at all."

"I don't think there's anything particularly funny," said Mr. Haddock, "about a woman deceiving her husband."

The Bottin shrugged his shoulders and Mr. Haddock returned once more to his liqueur and the problem of Hattie.

But he was again interrupted, this time by a loud blast from a cornet. He looked up and saw another woman—a stout woman, who, having blown a note of attention, was announcing something to the crowd. He looked to the Bottin for an explanation.

"She says," interrupted the Bottin, "that she's going to play a song about three young men—Raoul, Maurice, and Henri."

"On that cornet?" asked Mr. Haddock.

The Bottin nodded.

"It's a bit *risqué*," he added.

"I should think it would be," said Mr. Haddock.

"I mean the words of the song," explained the Bottin.

"Why?" asked Mr. Haddock. "Some more Gallic wit?"

"Well," said the Bottin, "you see, Raoul loves Maurice and is jealous of Henri ——"

"Don't be silly," said Mr. Haddock.

The lady took a deep breath and began.

"Does this go on all afternoon?" asked Mr. Haddock.

The Bottin nodded. "Off and on," he replied.

"Off," suggested Mr. Haddock, a little critically, "more than on."

But then Mr. Haddock was suddenly struck with a bright idea.

"How would it be," he said, "if we hire her to go around and play for Hattie? Maybe that will make her cheer up a bit."

"Fine," said the Bottin, "and the little girl might like it, too."

"Well, I'm not so sure about Mildred," said Mr. Haddock, "but anyway we can try."

So, when the lady had finished her solo and

the applause had died down, the Bottin called her over to his table and told her about the proposition.

"Ask her," said Mr. Haddock, "if she knows 'Nearer, My God, to Thee' and 'Way Down upon the Swanee River.' Those are Hattie's favorites. And no songs about anybody named Raoul."

The lady, when questioned about "Nearer, My God, to Thee," shook her head vigorously in the affirmative, so a price was agreed upon, and, after the three had had another round of drinks they started off for the concert.

"Shall she play in the street," asked the Bottin, "or in the room?"

"In the street will be better," replied Mr. Haddock, "at first. We can see how it goes."

When they reached the corner of Mr. Haddock's hotel they stopped just below Mrs. Haddock's window and the lady began to play the French version of Mrs. Haddock's favorite hymn.

"A good deal is lost," explained the Bottin, after one verse, "in the translation."

They waited for a few minutes, but there was no response from above.

"Have her play another one," said Mr. Haddock, "and I'll go up and see how it's going."

The lady played two or three more selections and then Mr. Haddock returned, shaking his head.

"It's not going," he said.

The lady shrugged her shoulders and busied herself in picking up various coins which people had flung from their windows, while Mr. Haddock and the Bottin went gloomily into consultation at a near-by café.

"I guess it's not entertainment that she needs," said Mr. Haddock at last, "so much as companionship. If she only had somebody to talk to!"

"I don't know any American women," said the Bottin.

"Hattie's met a Mrs. Ferguson," said Mr. Haddock, "and I know a Mrs. Abercrombie," and he suddenly looked at his watch. "By George! I was supposed to meet her at four o'clock."

Mr. and Mrs. Haddock

"Where?" asked the Bottin.

"At the Ritz bar," replied Mr. Haddock.

"You can make it," said the Bottin.

"Yes," said Mr. Haddock, "but I don't know whether I want to make it."

"What else is there to do?" asked the Bottin.

"That's just it," said Mr. Haddock. "I don't want to go back to that hotel and sit there and read guidebooks all afternoon."

"You'd better go to the Ritz," said the Bottin, "and I'll try to think up something before evening."

"What do you mean, something?" asked Mr. Haddock.

The Bottin stroked his beard and smiled.

"Well," he said, "perhaps I can think up a plan or two while you're away."

"Bottin," said Mr. Haddock, a little doubtfully, "are you sure I ought to go over to the Ritz?"

"Positive," said the Bottin.

So Mr. Haddock got in a taxicab and told the driver to go to the Ritz.

Once more he crossed the Seine to the right

[190]

bank. But this time, instead of going up the avenue toward the Opera House, the cab swung to the left, went past a gold statue of Joan of Arc on horseback, then along a row of shops, turned to the right, more shops, and then out into an open square, or rather circle, in the center of which was a large column.

"Vendôme," replied the driver in answer to Mr. Haddock's pointing.

In a few seconds they had swung around the column and arrived at the door of the Ritz.

It was fifteen minutes, though, before Mr. Haddock reached the bar, because, in the first place, there were so many mirrors that looked like doors; and in the second place, Mr. Haddock hated to ask questions; and in the third place, the bar was evidently to be reached only after a long walk through a long passageway which was lined with cases full of beautiful things for sale, and Mr. Haddock, on his way to meet Mrs. Abercrombie, found himself quite unexpectedly desirous of buying something very nice and appropriate to take home to his wife Harriet. He could not find anything, however, which seemed exactly in Hattie's line, and so he pressed on until he reached the end of the passageway which, after opening out into another lobby, led him at last to his intense relief, to the bar.

And there Mr. Haddock found a great many fine congenial Americans drinking and eating potato chips, and with their aid Mr. Haddock soon discovered something which came in a cocktail glass and was known as a "side car."

A well-dressed young man standing with his foot on the rail next to Mr. Haddock seemed to be especially friendly.

"Hurray!" he said, raising his glass to Mr. Haddock. "Hurray for Paris!"

"You like it here?" asked Mr. Haddock.

"Great," said the man. "Greatest place in the world."

"I haven't seen much of it yet," said Mr. Haddock. "Have you?"

"Sure," said the man, "seen everything— Luigi's, Ciro's, Zelli's, New York bar, Crillon bar. Seen everything," he repeated. "The best place in Paris to get Jack Rose's is at the Crillon," he added. "Get George to mix them. Do you know George?"

"No," admitted Mr. Haddock.

"The best bartender in Paris," said the young man.

The man on Mr. Haddock's left was even more enthusiastic.

"I found a joint," he said, "where you can get buckwheat cakes and real rye whisky."

"I used to put syrup on mine," said Mr. Haddock, "but I'm learning a lot over here."

"Let's sit down," said the man. "I've been standing here since three o'clock yesterday afternoon."

So they went over in a corner and took seats at a table.

"I'm from Chicago," announced the first gentleman, signaling the waiter, "and I'll take a champagne cocktail."

"I'm from Ohio," said Mr. Haddock. "The Buckeye State."

"Waiter," said the man, "got any drinks with buckeye in them?"

"No, sir," said the waiter.

"That's just like these French," said Mr. Haddock, pleasantly, "so I suppose I'll have to take a champagne cocktail, too. Will it mix with a 'side car'?"

"Sure," said the first. "Everything mixes in Paris. It's the climate."

"California's my state," said the other member of the party. "God's country."

"And what will the delegate from God's country have? Orange juice and gin?"

"I should say not," replied the Californian. "I came to Paris just to get away from orange juice and gin."

"So did I," admitted the first.

"I came to Paris," said Mr. Haddock, "to view the priceless monuments of the Old World, to bathe in the age-old splendor of a great civilization, to broaden myself," he concluded, with a gesture, "by contact with another race, another civilization, another—but I'll not say better—form of life."

"Hurray!" cried the other two. "And so you came to the Ritz bar."

"Well," admitted Mr. Haddock, "my coming here was more or less in the nature of an accident." And he excused himself for a minute and went out to see if Mrs. Abercrombie had yet appeared.

There were no signs of her, however, and he returned to his companions.

"You didn't see a rather tall woman out there, did you?" asked the Chicagoan, "dressed in black silk with a sort of green feather in her hat?"

"No," said Mr. Haddock, shaking his head.

"It's my wife," said the man. "She's looking for me," and he chuckled. "She's been looking for me since this morning."

"Why the hell did you bring your wife to Paris?" asked the Californian.

"Oh, we have a fine time," said the other. "She shops all day at those dressmakers and I drink all day, and at night we go on a big party together and both get stewed. Just like at home."

"Only the liquor's cheaper," said the other, "and better. Thank God for Paris, I say."

Mr. Haddock was silent. "I brought my wife, too," he said, finally, a little hesitantly, "and I'm having quite a time trying to keep her amused because there's nobody here for her to talk to. And she's quite a talker," he added, "when she gets started."

"That's too bad," said the man from California. "I knew a woman like that once."

"You never knew anyone like my wife," said Mr. Haddock. "She's the most wonderful little woman in the world." And he began reaching in his pocket for his passport picture.

"I tell you what," said the Chicago man, suddenly, "let's finish these drinks and then we'll all go over to the Café de la Paix and maybe somebody will walk by there that this gentleman knows and he can take her home for his wife to talk to."

"All right," said Mr. Haddock. "I don't think the party I was waiting for here is going to show up, anyway."

So they paid the check and filled their mouths with potato chips and left.

"Let's go back through the hotel," said the

[196]

Californian, "and walk up the Rue de la Paix."

"Not the famous Rue de la Paix?" said Mr. Haddock. "The most fashionable street in the world and the center of the shopping district of Paris?"

"The same," replied the other, and it was.

"They say," said the Chicagoan, as they found a table at the Café de la Paix and sat down, "that if you wait here long enough, everybody in the world will pass by."

"If I wait here that long," said Mr. Haddock, "I'll be pretty well stewed," and he gave a slight warning giggle.

Three drinks were ordered and the three men settled back to watch everybody in the world go by.

"I should think," said the Californian to the Chicagoan, "that you would be a little bit afraid of having your wife running around Paris all alone with these Frenchmen."

"As a matter of fact," said the Chicagoan, "I'm not too crazy about it."

"Frenchmen," said the other, "are not to be trusted a minute—not a minute."

"That's *one* thing," said Mr. Haddock, "that doesn't worry me," and he picked up his glass. Then he put it down very quickly and his eyes got very large.

The first person to pass the Café de la Paix was none other than Mr. Haddock's wife Hattie, and she was not alone. She was leaning on the arm of a bearded Frenchman and she was looking up into his face and smiling. It was the Bottin.

"Well, for Chr——" began Mr. Haddock.

"What's the matter?" asked the Chicagoan. "See somebody you know?"

Mr. Haddock took a deep breath.

"No," he replied, and by that time Hattie had passed on down the boulevard.

"Say," said Mr. Haddock, after a few minutes of reflective drinking, "do either of you men speak French?"

"Sure," said the man from Chicago. "Trays beans, garson—how's that?"

"I took French in college," said the Californian, "but a hell of a lot of good that does me over here."

"Well, can you tell me," asked Mr. Haddock, "what one word means?"

"What word?"

" 'Bottin,' " replied Mr. Haddock. "What's a Bottin? Has it got anything to do with women?"

The Californian shook his head. "No," he replied; "it's a kind of a city directory. *'Ici on consulte le Bottin'*—you mean that?"

"Yes," replied Mr. Haddock.

"Well, that's a city directory," said the Californian, "like you find in drug stores at home."

"I see," said Mr. Haddock, a little relieved. And after a few minutes he said good-by to the two gentlemen and started home.

But he didn't go home right away. There was much to be thought over in Mr. Haddock's mind, and he walked slowly along the boulevards without paying particular attention to where he was going.

There were a great many people hurrying along the boulevard, many of whom bumped into Mr. Haddock and most of whom politely said, *"Pardon."* Mr. Haddock passed several news stands kept by very old women, four or five moving-picture places, a shop where people were listening to phonograph records by placing tubes in their ears, some newspaper offices, and then finally he came to a large brownstone arch and, as he felt tired, sat down at another of those numerous cafés before trying to get a taxi.

"Come, Haddock, old fellow," he said to himself, "this will never do."

"What will never do?" asked the gentleman at the next table, looking up from his newspaper.

"This," replied Mr. Haddock, with an expansive gesture. "I mean, all this business of worrying about one's wife."

"Ah," replied the gentleman. "My card."

Mr. Haddock took the card and looked at it.

"Well, well!" he said. "So you're Lecocq, the famous French detective."

Mr. Lecocq bowed. "At your service," he said.

"Well," said Mr. Haddock, "it's this way. I was sitting at a café and when I looked up there was my wife walking along with another man—a Frenchman."

"Oh," said the detective. "You American husbands!"

"All right," said Mr. Haddock, "but even at that, what do we do next? I mean," he continued, "granted that I *am* only an American, what can you suggest?"

"Shadow!" replied the detective.

"Shadow?" asked Mr. Haddock.

"Precisely," replied the detective. "Shadow. Shadow your wife every minute of the day and night."

"But," began Mr. Haddock, "who ——"

"I," replied the detective, pointing to himself. "I am the most famous shadow in Paris —in the world. You doubt it?"

"No," replied Mr. Haddock.

"Yes, you do," said the detective. "All right. You doubt it. Then I must prove it to you. Will you kindly close your eyes and count twenty?"

[201]

Mr. Haddock closed his eyes and counted twenty, and when he opened them again the detective had disappeared and in his place sat an old man with a long gray beard.

"Guess who," said the old man in a high, shaky voice.

"Lecocq, the famous French detective," guessed Mr. Haddock.

"Oh, shoot!" said the detective. "You looked. Now shut your eyes again."

So Mr. Haddock complied. .

This time when he opened them Mr. Haddock saw an old, bent-over woman, probably an apple woman.

"Now who am I?" said the old woman.

"I give up," said Mr. Haddock.

"I am Lecocq," said the man, taking off his mask with a smile of triumph, "the famous French detective."

"Gosh!" said Mr. Haddock. "I never would have known you."

"Now to business," said the Frenchman, and Mr. Haddock reached for his pocketbook.

"You pay me five hundred francs and I'll

shadow your wife day and night and at the end of each twenty-four hours I give you a written report as to exactly where she has been and what she has done."

"Done," said Mr. Haddock.

"I said 'done,' " said the detective, a little peevishly. "Didn't I pronounce it right?"

"I meant 'agreed,' " said Mr. Haddock. "Your pronunciation is perfect."

"Have you a picture of your wife?" asked the detective.

"Not a very good one," said Mr. Haddock. "It's a passport picture." And he showed it to the other.

"Hmm," said the detective, gazing at it intently. "I would know her anywhere. And what is the address?"

Mr. Haddock gave him the address.

"From now on," said the detective, "I'll follow your wife like a hawk."

"A nice hawk," said Mr. Haddock, "because she's really a very nice woman and I'm just curious."

[203]

So the two men shook hands and Mr. Haddock left in search of a taxicab.

He finally found one, but just as he was getting in, he was stopped by a tap on the shoulder and he turned to see an old Jewish trinket salesman who was evidently trying to sell him trinkets.

"Trinkets?" said the salesman.

"No trinkets," replied Mr. Haddock.

The salesman laughed. "Don't you know me?" he said.

Mr. Haddock looked again.

"I remember your face," he said. "Didn't we meet at the banquet in honor of Governor Herrick?"

"No," said the man, shaking his head. "I am Lecocq."

"Amazing," said Mr. Haddock, holding up his hands. "Colossal."

"I'm glad you like it," said the detective, visibly pleased, "and this is just the beginning," and with a happy smile he disappeared into a convenient French comfort station and Mr. Haddock drove on.

When Mr. Haddock got home he paused for a minute outside his door and listened. Then he knocked.

"Come in," said Mrs. Haddock, after a minute. Mr. Haddock opened the door and entered. He sniffed. There was a strange perfume in the room—an Oriental scent.

"Why, what did you knock for?" asked Mrs. Haddock.

Mr. Haddock shrugged his shoulders and laughed. "There's many a knock," said Mr. Haddock, significantly, " 'twixt the cup and the lip."

"There's many a *what?*" said Mrs. Haddock, and she came up and smelled his breath.

"I thought so," she said.

"*You* thought so," said Mr. Haddock. "Well, what do you suppose I thought?"

"About what?" asked Mrs. Haddock.

"Oh, the mockery of it all," said Mr. Haddock.

"Will Haddock!" said Mrs. Haddock, "where in Heaven's name have you been?"

Mr. Haddock was silent.

[205]

"How is our child?" he asked. "Our little Mildred."

"Our Mildred!" said Mrs. Haddock. "*Our* Mildred!" she repeated.

"Then she isn't our Mildred," said Mr. Haddock, and he laughed ironically.

"One more day of Paris," said Mrs. Haddock, "and you'll drive me crazy."

"Hello, father," called Mildred from the other room.

"She's much better," said Mrs. Haddock. "I think she can get up to-morrow."

Mr. Haddock crossed over into Mildred's room and was greeted with a pillow in his face.

"Look, father," she cried, "I'm almost well."

Mr. Haddock kissed her affectionately.

"See what I brought you," he said.

"Oh, what?" cried the little girl.

Mr. Haddock reached in all his pockets.

"I guess I forgot to get it."

Mildred laughed.

"No, honest," said her father. "I meant

to get you something and then something else happened."

"What happened?" asked little Mildred.

Mr. Haddock put his finger to his lips. "Shhh!" he said, for Mrs. Haddock was at that moment coming into the room.

But suddenly Mr. Haddock detected, or thought he detected, a swift look of understanding pass between mother and daughter, and he even seemed to see Mildred's left eye close in an unmistakable wink.

"What is this," he cried in despair, "some vast, great, enormous conspiracy or other?"

"Why, what do you mean?" said Mrs. Haddock.

Mr. Haddock lapsed into silence.

"Nothing," he said. "Less than nothing."

The telephone rang. Mrs. Haddock, almost too eagerly, Mr. Haddock thought, ran to answer it.

"It's your friend, the Bottin," she announced.

"*My* friend!" said Mr. Haddock. "Ha, ha, ha."

"Yes," replied his wife. "He wants to know if you need him this evening."

"Do you?" asked Mr. Haddock.

"Do I what?" said his wife.

"Do you need the Bottin this evening?"

"Why, no," replied Mrs. Haddock. "I'm going to stay here with Mildred."

"Then I'll stay, too," said Mr. Haddock.

"Oh, father," said little Mildred, "don't do that. You really ought to get out more."

"That's right, Will," said Mrs. Haddock.

Mr. Haddock looked from one woman to the other suspiciously.

"That's awfully good of you," he said, "but I think I'll stay right here."

So Mrs. Haddock told the Bottin to telephone again in the morning.

Dinner arrived.

"To-morrow," announced Mrs. Haddock, "I want you to remain here with Mildred, Will."

"But I want to go out to-morrow myself," cried little Mildred, "and see Paris. Please, mamma!"

Mrs. Haddock shook her head.

"The doctor says ——"

"Oh, to hell with the doctor."

"Mildred!" said Mrs. Haddock. "People don't talk that way about doctors. And please pass mother the celery."

Mr. Haddock regarded his wife thoughtfully.

"Going out alone, dear?" he asked.

"No," replied Mrs. Haddock.

"Oh," said her husband. "I see," and, after a few minutes, "With Mrs. Ferguson, perhaps?"

"No," said Mrs. Haddock.

"I see," said Mr. Haddock, and there was another silence.

"I'm going out," announced Mrs. Haddock, "with Mr. Bottin."

"Ah, yes," said Mr. Haddock, "that fellow. Well, well! A very nice chap, I believe."

"I want to do some sight-seeing," explained Mrs. Haddock.

"I'm very glad," said Mr. Haddock, "and I'm sure you'll be in very good hands."

Mrs. Haddock did not reply.

"Mamma," asked little Mildred, looking up from her bowl of crackers and milk, "is papa *cocu* yet?"

"Is papa *what?*"

"*Cocu,*" repeated the little girl, and she explained what it meant in French.

Mrs. Haddock blushed.

"Mildred," she said, "you go right in to bed."

"But I just wanted to know," said Mildred, "and so does papa."

Mrs. Haddock looked at her husband.

"Why, Will Haddock," she said, "of all things," and she gave a little giggle.

"Come on," urged little Mildred. "Tell us about it."

"Mildred," said her father, "you go to bed."

"I should say not," said the little girl, and she drew her knees up in the chair and looked at her mother with eager anticipation.

"Mr. Bottin," said Mrs. Haddock, recovering her dignity, "is a very nice gentleman."

"Of course," said little Mildred. "They always are."

"Hattie," said Mr. Haddock. "For Heaven's sake, what have you been up to?"

"Mr. Bottin," said Mrs. Haddock, "very kindly came up this afternoon and asked me if I would like to take a little walk around Paris."

"Yes," said little Mildred, "and then what?"

"If that man," said Mr. Haddock, "harms a hair of your head ———"

Mrs. Haddock smoothed her hair reflectively and smiled.

"Mr. Bottin," she continued, "is French."

"Oh, come on, mamma," cried little Mildred. "We know that. But what happened?"

"Frenchmen," said Mrs. Haddock, patiently, "are different. They look at things differently from the way American men do."

Mr. Haddock bit off the end of a cigar.

"And so ———"

"Yes?" said little Mildred, eagerly.

"And so Mr. Bottin and I took a little taxi ride and had tea and then came home."

"Fire's out," said Mildred, disappointedly.

"Was anything wrong about that?" asked Mrs. Haddock.

"Of course not," replied her husband. "And, of course, Hattie, I trust you implicitly. And the only thing I was really thinking about all the time was little Mildred, our little girl, left all alone here in this hotel—sick, helpless——"

"They got Mrs. Ferguson to come in," explained Mildred. "She stunk the place all up with some kind of French perfume, too."

Mr. Haddock said nothing.

"And so you're going out again to-morrow," he asked, "with that foreigner?"

"Why, of course, Will!" replied Mrs. Haddock. "He knows all about Paris."

"Hmmm," said Mr. Haddock, and he lapsed into silence.

About nine o'clock, Mrs. Haddock said that she felt sleepy and thought she would go to bed, and about half-past ten Mr. Haddock yawned, put down the guidebook he was reading, and followed suit.

CHAPTER IX

AND about four thirty in the morning both Mr. and Mrs. Haddock were awakened by the ringing of the telephone bell. Mr. Haddock finally found one slipper and his bathrobe and answered it.

"Mr. Haddock?" came the voice over the wire, a very excited voice.

"Yes," he replied.

"I've got your wife," said the voice, "and we're holding her."

It was Lecocq, of the French Secret Service.

Mr. Haddock glanced at Mrs. Haddock and replied, "Are you sure?"

"Yes," came the answer, "and you had better come right away."

"Who is it, Will?" asked Mrs. Haddock.

"It's a man," replied Mr. Haddock.

"Will Haddock," said his wife, "you come back to bed."

"No," said Mr. Haddock, firmly, reaching for his trousers. "I've got to get to the bottom of this. How do I know," he added, "that that is *you* there in bed?" and he pinched his wife to make sure. "How do I know *anything* any more since I've come over here abroad."

"Will!" said Mrs. Haddock. "You're crazy as a loon."

But her protests were of no avail and in ten minutes Mr. Haddock was in a taxicab speeding rapidly toward the address which Lecocq had given him.

It was a wild ride, but a great deal of Paris at five o'clock in the morning was comparatively asleep. Mr. Haddock passed an occasional market wagon piled high with carrots or other vegetables, and here and there were to be seen a few cafés still open. It was just beginning to get light, and in the pale, early morning Mr. Haddock suddenly noticed that they were crossing the river and then, right before his eyes, loomed the two towers of a very large cathedral which Mr. Haddock, to his astonishment, recognized as Notre Dame.

It somehow didn't seem right to Mr. Haddock to be looking at Notre Dame this closely when he wasn't on a sight-seeing tour, but he couldn't help admitting, nevertheless, that it was a very impressive church, even if it didn't seem quite as big as he had expected.

He had no idea where they were going, and he began to doubt if the taxi driver did. In a few minutes, however, they pulled up opposite the door of a café, and as Mr. Haddock was climbing out of the cab a dark, mysterious figure which had been loitering under a lamp post suddenly slouched toward him. Mr. Haddock stuck out his hand and said, cheerfully:

"Hello, Lecocq!"

"Shh!" said Lecocq. "Not so loud. And how did you recognize me?"

"I didn't," said Mr. Haddock.

"Good," said Lecocq, and he led his client over to a table, where they sat down.

"Now," he said in a whisper, "your wife's

[215]

in there," and he jerked his head in the direction of the interior of the café.

"What's she doing?" asked Mr. Haddock.

"Eating onion soup," replied the detective.

"My God!" said Mr. Haddock. "I'm glad you called me."

"Precisely," said the detective, pulling out a report, "and here is the exact summary of her movements since she left the hotel at eight fourteen this evening."

Mr. Haddock examined the report with much interest.

"How did you know it was my wife?" he asked.

"By the passport picture," replied Lecocq, "and by certain other indications which only a detective would know."

"And you mean to say," went on Mr. Haddock, pointing to the report, "that she's been to *all* these places this evening?"

"Yes," replied Lecocq. "And I will say, Mr. Haddock, that your wife has certainly a wonderful constitution."

"Well, for example," said Mr. Haddock, pointing to an item, "what's that?"

The detective looked. "That's Zelli's," he said. "She went there at twelve fourteen and stayed until three nine."

"What doing?" asked Mr. Haddock.

"Drinking champagne," replied the detective, "and dancing."

"By the way," asked Mr. Haddock, "whom was she with all this time?"

"Several gentlemen," replied the detective, and he consulted another report.

"The first one passed out at twelve thirty-six; the next two became exhausted and dropped at one eleven and one fifty-eight, respectively. That left two. They're both in there now."

A woman's laugh sounded inside.

"Shh!" said the detective. "They may be coming out."

He was right—or rather, he was partly right. The lady appeared, alone. She was in evening dress, with a large, beautiful Spanish shawl thrown around her shoulders.

It was Mrs. Abercrombie, of Pittsburgh.

"Oh, hello!" she said. "You're just in time."

"Time for what?" asked Mr. Haddock.

"To go swimming," she said, "in the Seine— They say it's great fun. And then we're going to the markets and get some more onion soup, and then ——"

"Yes," interrupted Mr. Haddock, "and then?"

"And then," finished Mrs. Abercrombie, "we can go for a drive in the Bois. It's going to be a heavenly morning."

"Isn't it, though," said Mr. Haddock.

"You wait out here," said Mrs. Abercrombie, "and I'll go back and wake Joe and Mr. Fisher up. They've been asleep for the last half hour."

When she had disappeared, the detective spoke.

"Well," he said, "what about it?"

"Great," replied Mr. Haddock, "only she isn't my wife."

The detective seemed stunned.

"Why, you're crazy!" he said. "She is, too, your wife."

"No, honest," replied Mr. Haddock, "and you don't know how relieved I am."

"But she looks like the picture," insisted the detective.

"That may well be," said Mr. Haddock, "but she's much younger." He was suddenly struck with a curious idea. "Say," he said, "that is sort of funny, too, isn't it. She *does* look a little like Hattie—or rather, she looks like Hattie used to look before she took on weight. You know," he concluded, "I *thought* there was some reason why she seemed so doggoned pretty to me."

Mrs. Abercrombie returned, leading two very tired and weary Americans in evening clothes.

"Come on," she cried, starting ahead, "we're going to walk along the Seine until we come to a good swimming place."

She began running and skipping very gracefully and very energetically along the *quai*.

The one American looked at the other American and groaned.

"Oh, my God!" he said.

The two men gazed at each other for a minute and then both must have gotten the same idea at once, for suddenly, without a word, they turned and began running in the opposite direction as fast as they could.

The lady stopped under a lamp post and beckoned.

"It seems to be up to me," said Mr. Haddock.

"What about me?" asked the great French detective.

"I'm paying you," said Mr. Haddock, "to watch my wife, not me."

The detective bowed. "Very good, sir," he said. "I'll report in the morning." And in a twinkling of his eye he had disappeared into another convenient French comfort station.

When Mr. Haddock had caught up with Mrs. Abercrombie he was puffing slightly, although he tried hard to conceal it.

"I'm afraid," she said, "that none of the

swimming places will be open yet. Let's just walk along for a while and breathe Paris."

So Mrs. Abercrombie and Mr. Haddock walked along, breathing Paris.

"Paris is great," she said, "isn't it?"

A few of the bargemen in the river were already beginning their day's work, or whatever it is that bargemen begin, and smoke was coming from one or two of the large, red scows anchored along the bank. Then, in a little while, the two Americans had reached the short island-to-island bridge, and there was Notre Dame again, more beautiful and more impressive than ever from the rear in the lovely light of a Paris dawn.

In the large square in front of the cathedral Mr. Haddock, to his joy, discovered a solitary open victoria, and when they had waked the cabman up he got in beside Mrs. Abercrombie. She gave some directions to the driver in French and they slowly started off.

"First," she said, "we'll go to the markets."

The carriage rattled over the Paris streets, across the bridge to the right bank, and then before long they found themselves jogging slowly between sidewalks heaped high with carrots, cabbages, melons, flowers—everything.

"This smells good, too," said Mr. Haddock.

The sun, by now, was up. Mr. Haddock stopped the vehicle, got out, and bought a large bunch of roses from an old woman who smiled her thanks at them and threw in an extra bouquet for good luck. Market women watched as the carriage rattled past; some yelled hoarse, indistinguishable, good-natured greetings.

"The sweet old dears," said Mrs. Abercrombie.

The driver up in front, a solitary, morose figure in a very old coat and a shiny, patent-leather high hat, cracked his whip from time to time and spoke to the horse, which, as Mr. Haddock remarked, was evidently the last horse left in Paris after the heavy rains of 1903.

"Don't you love it all?" said the lady, and

Mr. Haddock, holding her hand, nodded his assent.

"To the Bois," she said to the driver, and after a short argument about additional money they started for the Bois.

Paris by now was gradually waking up. Carts were rumbling over the streets; cafés were opening; men were drinking coffee out in front; taxicabs were becoming more numerous.

They drove slowly along beside the Louvre, past the gardens of the Tuileries, and into the Place de la Concorde. The horse's hoofs sounded very sharp and clear as they swung around into the Avenue de Champs Élysées.

At the Arc de Triomphe, they chose one of the roads leading out from the other side, and in a few minutes they were in the Bois.

Mr. Haddock had never seen such beautiful trees and such a beautiful park since his last trip to Kansas City, and even that began to seem a little insignificant as they drove on and on past small lakes and race courses and a very large grand stand.

"Longchamps," said the lady.

Finally Mr. Haddock sighed and looked at his watch.

"I've got to be getting back," he said.

The lady looked at him and smiled.

"Why?" she asked, and there didn't seem to be any answer.

"This Paris is a funny place," said Mr. Haddock, half to himself. "And the more I see of it the funnier it gets. Here I am, for example, driving around in a strange carriage with a strange lady in evening clothes at seven thirty in the morning; and yet it all seems perfectly natural and perfectly right.

"But just the same," he said, after a few minutes, "I'd better be getting back."

"All right," said the lady. "Where do you go?"

Mr. Haddock told her.

So she spoke to the driver, and after a while they were once more driving over the Paris streets in the direction of the Hôtel de New York et Sainte-Agnes.

"Aren't you going to bed," asked Mr. Haddock, "and get some sleep?"

The lady laughed.

"Go to bed in Paris?" she said. "I should say not."

At the hotel entrance Mr. Haddock said good-by, and stood for a minute watching the carriage as Mrs. Abercrombie drove out of his life forever. Then he went in.

Mrs. Haddock was waiting for him with her hat on.

"Look, dear," said Mr. Haddock, "I've brought you some flowers from the markets," and he handed her an enormous bouquet. "And you can't guess where I've been," he added.

"No," said Mrs. Haddock, "I can't."

So Mr. Haddock tried to describe to her how wonderful Paris was in the early morning. They were interrupted by the telephone.

"All right," said Mrs. Haddock. "Tell him I'll be right down."

Mr. Haddock said nothing.

"Good-by," said Mrs. Haddock, "and don't let Mildred have more than two pieces of that candy after lunch."

Mr. Haddock stood watching his wife as she went out the door. In a minute she came back.

"I forgot my gloves," she said.

She found her gloves and was gone.

Mr. Haddock walked to the window and watched. Mrs. Haddock came out on to the sidewalk; she was accompanied by the Bottin. They started up the street, evidently in search of a taxicab.

And then from out a near-by doorway a figure darted—a figure wrapped in a long black cape and a black slouch hat. He dodged behind a lamp post, ran forward into another doorway, and then out again.

Mr. Haddock felt somewhat relieved.

He pulled down the shades, looked in at little Mildred, who was reading quietly in bed, talked to her for a little while about how beautiful Paris was in the early morning, and then, feeling quite tired and sleepy, he lay down on his own bed and closed his eyes.

When he woke up it was late afternoon. He jumped hastily to his feet. Mrs. Haddock had not yet returned.

"Mildred," called Mr. Haddock.

There was no answer.

"Mildred!" he called again, and then rushed through the intervening door into his daughter's room.

Mildred was gone.

Mr. Haddock ran to the window. There was nothing to be seen. He tore back into his own room and reached for the telephone. He rattled the hook desperately up and down.

There was no answer.

Suddenly Mr. Haddock looked up, and his eye was caught by a white envelope stuck in the mirror. His heart momentarily stopped beating. Hattie. Like in the movies.

With trembling hands he slowly reached for the envelope, opened it and read:

"Dear father: I've gone out to see Paris." It was signed, "Your loving daughter, Mildred B. Haddock."

Then there was a postscript. "P.S.," it said, "I only took two pieces of candy."

Mr. Haddock began to picture to himself the various pitfalls and terrors of this French city. And his daughter was out there, all alone, in the midst of an alien population who might be capable of almost anything. Defenseless.

He was reaching for his hat when suddenly in the street below he heard a most terrible howl. He rushed to the window, his heart in his mouth.

But it was not Mildred.

It was a little French boy and he was running up the street, crying as though his heart would break. He disappeared into a doorway.

Heads began to appear at windows. Two more little boys came running from the same direction, with the same pitiful appearance; one of the boys was limping as he ran, and the other's face seemed to be badly scratched.

There was a moment of silence.

Then around the corner came Mildred, a little belligerently, but very happy.

Mr. Haddock grinned.

"Lafayette," he said, "we are here."

In a few more minutes Mildred opened the door softly and came in.

"Where have you been?" asked her father.

"Seeing Paris," replied Mildred. "Didn't you get my note?"

Mr. Haddock grinned again. "How do you like Paris?" he asked.

"It's all right," replied little Mildred, "except for the people. Where's mother? Isn't she back yet?"

Mr. Haddock shook his head.

"It's almost six o'clock," he said, "and she was only going to be gone till noon."

There was the noise of a taxi driving up outside the hotel, and little Mildred ran to the window.

"It's an old man getting out," she said. "No, he's not so old, either. He just seems to be very tired."

"Is he alone?" asked Mr. Haddock.

"Yes," replied Mildred.

"Well," said her father, "the only thing we can do is wait."

In a few minutes there was a knock at the door. Mr. Haddock ran and opened it.

There stood Lecocq.

"That's the man," said little Mildred, "that got out of the taxicab."

"Mr. Haddock," said Lecocq, immediately, "I would like to resign."

"Why, what's the matter?" asked Mr. Haddock.

Lecocq came feebly into the room and sank on the edge of the bed.

"Your wife," he announced, "has been sight-seeing," and he took from his pocket another of his report blanks.

"Since nine o'clock this morning," he said, "I have shadowed her faithfully and patiently and I would like to resign."

"Why?" asked Mr. Haddock.

The detective glanced at the report.

"Since nine o'clock," he said, "your wife has visited three museums, seven churches, the national library, the national archives, the Jardin des Plantes, the Jardin d'Acclimation, five department stores, Napoleon's tomb and the Louvre. I left her," he concluded, "as she was entering the Père-Lachaise Cemetery."

"Was the Bottin still with her?" asked Mr. Haddock.

"The Bottin," replied the detective, "dropped out after the second church."

Mr. Haddock smiled, and breathed a sigh of relief.

"Good old Hattie," he said.

The detective groaned.

"I'm sorry," said Mr. Haddock, "that you feel like resigning, but still ——"

"Mr. Haddock," said Lecocq, "I'm getting on in years. I'm not as young as I used to be, and if I had to do any more of that god damned sight-seeing ——"

Mr. Haddock laughed.

"All right," he said. "We'll call it a day."

It was ten minutes later that Mrs. Haddock arrived. Her hands were full of postcards and souvenir guidebooks. Her feet dragged a little wearily, but in her eyes was a gleam of triumph.

"I've done over half of it, Will," she announced, "and I'm sure I can finish it tomorrow."

"We're all very proud of you," said Mr. Haddock, "and people back home will be proud, too. We were a little worried," he added, "when you didn't come home at noon."

"Didn't you get my telephone message?"

"No," replied Mr. Haddock, "but it doesn't matter now."

"Has Mildred been a good girl?" asked Mrs. Haddock.

Mr. Haddock smiled. "Very," he replied, patting his daughter on the head.

"If she gets to bed early," said Mrs. Haddock, "I'm sure it will be all right for her to see Paris to-morrow."

"And then," said Mr. Haddock, "we could leave on Friday. Why not go out to-night," he added, "and have a little party in honor of Mildred's getting well?"

"No," replied Mrs. Haddock. "You know, I'm kind of tired, Will."

"Lecocq would be happy to hear that," said Mr. Haddock.

"Who?"

"Oh, just a man who used to work for me,"

replied her husband. "Come on, let's ring for the waiter."

So dinner was once more served in the hotel room.

The Haddocks retired early in preparation for their last day in Paris.

Mr. Haddock tried to go to sleep; the taxicabs in the street below kept him awake. Or perhaps it was the filet mignon. He lay there under that sheet as quietly as he could, staring at that strange ceiling and thinking about Paris.

So much had happened. It seemed a long time ago.

Mr. Haddock wanted to come to some definite conclusion about the past four days. He wanted to be able to say that Paris was so and so and that the French were definitely this and that.

And not only Paris and the French. The Belgians, too, and the English. That Russian on the bridge. There is no God. Mrs. Abercrombie. Mrs. Ferguson. Americans. The Ritz. Americans in Paris.

"What is it, Will?" asked Mrs. Haddock.

"Nothing, dear."

"You groaned."

"It's hot in here."

There was no answer.

Mr. Haddock tried counting sheep.

As sheep number two jumped over the stile, Mr. Haddock thought of the Bottin. St.-Germain-des-Prés. Notre Dame. The markets. The Bois. Mrs. Abercrombie again. Mrs. Haddock. The Bottin.

He lifted up the sheet, sat quietly erect, and felt for his slippers.

"Where are you going, Will?"

"Just out."

"Out where?"

"Oh, out. I want to walk around a bit."

The street was quiet and deserted as he walked along. And then the more he thought about it, the more he wanted to talk to somebody about all these things. Maybe somebody else could give him the answer.

Mr. Haddock found the Bottin at the Café des Deux Magots.

"Hello!" said the Bottin, putting down his liqueur and wiping his beard.

"Hello!" said Mr. Haddock. "Doing anything?"

The Bottin shook his head.

Mr. Haddock sat down and ordered a beer.

"How is Mrs. Haddock?" asked the Bottin.

Mr. Haddock did not reply.

"Look, Bottin," he said at last, "I've come to a decision. I think you French are all wrong."

"About what?"

Mr. Haddock's beer arrived and he took a long drink before replying.

"About women," he said.

The Bottin took a cigarette out of a yellow packet and lighted it slowly with a sulphur match.

"Tell me, Haddock," he asked, "just what do you know about the French, anyway?"

"Well," replied Mr. Haddock, after deliberating a minute, "I know you. And I've read books, and seen plays on the stage."

"In which the Frenchman," interrupted the

Bottin, "is always a devil with the women and says 'Ooo-la-la.'"

"Now listen, Bottin," objected Mr. Haddock. "You aren't going to go on and tell me about the battle of the Marne, are you, when civilization wavered?"

The Bottin smiled.

"No," he replied. "All I'm suggesting is that Americans ought to know more about the real France and the real French people before they go around talking about 'the French.'"

"Well, for that matter," said Mr. Haddock, "I've met Frenchmen who think that all Americans are millionaires who spend their time shooting buffaloes out of skyscraper windows."

"I know it," said the Bottin. "You can't tell me anything about that. The French are in many respects the most ignorant, most self-satisfied people in the world. But," he added, "they aren't like the Americans think they are."

"I don't know *what* I think," said Mr. Haddock; "it's all so sort of confusing over here.

Nothing is right —— Look at that, for example, Bottin."

Mr. Haddock was pointing to the opposite sidewalk, where a middle-aged, bearded Frenchman was walking by, kissing his female companion on the lips as they promenaded.

"In public like that," said Mr. Haddock; "and look over there."

A young French girl had just seated herself at a table. She was accompanied by a large, black, well-dressed negro.

"And this afternoon," continued Mr. Haddock, "Mrs. Haddock saw a French mother, while the traffic was going on, hold her baby out in a sitting position over the gutter. And those public what-do-you-call-'ems on every corner. I'm asking you, Bottin, what sort of a place is this, anyway?"

The Bottin did not reply, and Mr. Haddock continued.

"All right, Bottin," he said, "I'm open-minded, see? Let's leave morals out of it for a while. I came over here to have a good time and to give Hattie and Mildred a good time, which God knows, for some reason, I haven't succeeded in doing. But anyway, I also came over to learn something, too. I'm curious, see? I always have been. About everything. I want to learn.

"Well," continued Mr. Haddock, "I've learned a lot. I've learned, for one thing, that no matter what the newspapers say, the French don't like the Americans, and the English don't like the Americans, and I bet the Germans and Italians don't either—and anybody that says so is just a blind blithering fool.

"Sure," he went on, as though the Bottin had denied it, "they *say* they like us—and they take our *money* gladly enough—and tell us we're great when it comes to donating funds for the Red Cross or some earthquake or war or something—but down in their hearts they despise us. Now look, Bottin," said Mr. Haddock, "I'm asking you. Why is that?"

The Bottin did not reply.

"And another thing," went on Mr. Haddock, "why don't we Americans like the French? Here you've got a wonderful city—

honest, Bottin, it is beautiful as hell. There's something about it—just sitting here, for example, and looking at that church over there; it does something to you. And life here must be great. But just the same," he went on, "I don't like the people. The women don't look right, somehow; they don't seem open-air, if you know what I mean. They all look as if they *knew* too much. And the men—listen, Bottin," he said, "why is it that I want to sock most of the men when they begin talking and waving their arms? And why is it, Bottin, that I know damned well that we Americans are going to lick all you Europeans some day? I know we can do it and by God! Bottin, I think *you* know it in your hearts—and that's why you despise us so. It's fear."

"Was it fear," asked the Bottin, after a minute, "that built that church over there?"

Mr. Haddock considered.

"No," he replied, "but look, Bottin, that church is dead—or rather the people who built it are dead—long ago. And America is alive."

"Are you building churches?" asked the Bottin.

"There are more churches in Legion, Ohio," replied Mr. Haddock, "than in any town of its size in the state."

"Yes," said the Bottin, "but what kind of churches?"

Mr. Haddock did not reply.

"Haddock," said the Bottin, "I'm going to tell you something about America. Some of us over here know it perhaps better than most of you do yourselves. And a great deal that you have said to-night, both about France and America, is true—too ghastly true to be funny."

He lighted another cigarette.

"Because," he went on, "the more you know about America the more you come to appreciate that it *is* a young country—and the more you see of Europe the more you are apt to realize that it is an *old* country—and perhaps too old, too tired, to ever get up again and walk.

"But at the same time," he continued, "Europe isn't dead yet—not by a long sight. And Americans can learn a lot from Europe if they will only grow up—and stop boasting and acting like children.

"You see, Haddock," said the Bottin, "it isn't a question of America *licking* Europe—or Americans being *better* than Europeans—all that doesn't get you anywhere except where it has gotten the Germans and the French——

"But what *is* important," he went on, "is that America and Americans find their own soul—the American soul—because the soul of Europe right now," he said, "is very sick—and is looking for guidance.

"And that guidance," he said, "may come from you—or it may come from the East—I mean India. Or perhaps Russia. But it won't come from America until America finds itself—until everything alive in that country—skyscrapers, subways, farms, grain elevators, Ford factories, steel—reaches up simultaneously—higher—and finds its soul—and if that happens—if America flowers—powerfully, overwhelmingly, beautifully—

[241]

there will come a new religion—or a great rebirth of the old religion—and people will once more build churches which will be great beautiful churches because in them will be the expression of the great beautiful soul of this commercial industrial scientific age which is our own—and which is now groping so blindly in the dark—in America.

"And that," concluded the Bottin, "has somehow got something to do with you and Mrs. Haddock and the Americans, because you're all over here looking for something— something you're not getting in America. You don't know what it is but you think maybe it's over here, in Europe, and then you get sore when you don't find it."

Mr. Haddock puffed his cigar thoughtfully.

"Is Hattie unhappy?" he asked at length.

"Well," said the Bottin, "no. She's not actively unhappy. But she's not happy, either. There were so many things that she had hoped Paris was going to be and there were so many things that she had hoped it was going to do to her. She knew she wasn't having a good time and she knew that you wanted her to have a good time, and yet she just couldn't do it. She had never learned how."

Mr. Haddock nodded.

"That's the trouble," said the Bottin. "So many Americans are just like Mrs. Haddock —they don't know how to play. They work and work and work and they think that some day when they've accumulated enough money they'll go somewhere—Paris, Palm Beach, anywhere but where they are—and enjoy life. And the terrible thing is that it is *always too late.*"

Mr. Haddock did not speak for a long time.

"Say listen, Bottin," he said, finally, "all this has been great. I mean, it's great stuff. I didn't understand a lot of it, of course—especially that about the soul of America—but it sounded great. There's just one thing," he went on, "I want to ask you."

The Bottin, trembling a little with emotion, gravely nodded his head and lighted a cigarette.

"Well," continued Mr. Haddock, "honest to

God, now, Bottin, how about you and my wife?"

The Bottin suddenly threw back his head and laughed.

"Haddock," he said, "you're wonderful."

"I know it," said Mr. Haddock, "but I just sort of wanted to know. You're a younger man, Bottin. And you're French. And they do say that the women fall for Frenchmen, no matter what the age."

The Bottin looked into Mr. Haddock's eyes.

"Haddock," he said, "I'll tell you a secret."

Mr. Haddock said, "What?" a little doubtfully.

"Listen, Haddock," said the Bottin, "I'm not French."

"You're not French?"

"No," said the Bottin. "I'm an American."

"Well, I'll be damned," said Mr. Haddock.

"And what's more," continued the Bottin, "I come from your home town; I used to live in Legion."

"Oh, now listen," cried Mr. Haddock, bitterly. "This is just terrible. All the French-

women I've met come from Pittsburgh or
Cleveland or Toledo, and now you say you
lived in Legion."

"Third Street," continued the Bottin.

"Oh, hell!" said Mr. Haddock. "What's
the use."

He sank back in his chair dejectedly.

"Well," he said at last, "it's a small world."

"I haven't been back," said the Bottin, "for
twenty-two years."

"It's changed a lot," said Mr. Haddock.

"So have I," said the Bottin.

The two men sat for a long time without
speaking.

"Bottin," said Mr. Haddock, suddenly,
"what's it all about?"

"What's what all about?"

"It," replied Mr. Haddock. "This," and he
waved his hand in a comprehensive gesture.
"You—me—Paris—that church over there—
Legion, Ohio—America ——"

The Bottin was silent.

"Haddock," he said at last, "let's get
drunk."

Mr. and Mrs. Haddock

"All right," said Mr. Haddock. And then after a minute he added, "But just one thing, Bottin."

"Yes?"

"Don't ever tell Hattie you're not a Frenchman," said Mr. Haddock, "because," he added, with a smile, "I think ——"

"I understand," said the Bottin.

So Mr. Haddock and the Bottin slowly got very, very drunk, and when it was past midnight and the café was closing, Mr. Haddock insisted on having the Bottin go home with him and sleep with him, just to show Mrs. Haddock that everything was all right.

But when they got to the room, Mrs. Haddock refused to listen to any of their arguments about the world and God and where the *Titanic* was. So, after shaking hands several times and saying good-by several times, Mr. Haddock and the Bottin parted.

And then Mr. Haddock got very sick at his stomach.

[246]

CHAPTER X

MR. and Mrs. Haddock's last day in Paris began with a shopping tour.

"I want something," explained Mrs. Haddock to the very polite head manager of a large department store called the "Galeries Lafayette," "for my son Frank's wife—something French, but not too expensive. She has almost everything because she got a great many wedding presents from Frank's school friends, although some of them were duplicates and had to be exchanged except the ones that were marked with her initials, *F. B.,* which, of course, she couldn't exchange. And she had a birthday only last month and Frank gave her a Dodge sedan."

"*Oui,* madam."

So Mrs. Haddock bought Frank's wife a nice bead bag, and after looking carefully for something equally distinctively Parisian for Frank they bought him a French briar pipe.

"Now," said Mrs. Haddock, consulting her list, "that leaves only Uncle Walter, Cousin Walter, Aunt Caroline, Second Cousin Charlotte, the Guthrie twins, Tom Slocum, Mr. and Mrs. Ellis, Mr. and Mrs. Horace Doolittle, Mrs. Dobbie, the Torrence girls, Della the cook, Maggie, Maggie's baby, Miss Keating, the boys at your office and Gus. Can you think of anybody else?" she asked.

"President Coolidge," replied Mr. Haddock, leaning a little weakly against a lamp post, "and the Sixty-third Congress."

And by the time they finished it was almost one o'clock.

"If we're going to do any sight-seeing," said Mr. Haddock, "we'd better get some lunch."

So they went to a place recommended by Mrs. Jenkins, called "Prunier's," where the Haddocks were allowed to taste their first French oysters.

"Possibly," said Mr. Haddock, as he

thoughtfully put the oyster back on its half shell, "it's an acquired taste."

"You ordered them, Will," said Mrs. Haddock, "and you ought to eat them." And she carefully ate every one of hers.

But the rest of the meal was very good and they reached the boulevard just as the sight-seeing auto bus was starting. Mildred, Mr. Haddock, and Mrs. Haddock found places in the front seat directly facing the announcer, who was bald but was wearing a black rain-coat.

This latter gentleman, curiously enough, seemed slightly nervous. He kept glancing at Mr. Haddock as though he were trying to find out whether Mr. Haddock was the kind of a man he could trust; then just before time for starting he suddenly leaned over, plucked Mr. Haddock's sleeve, and said, "Psst!"

Mr. Haddock looked around.

"Psst!" said the man again.

He climbed down off the bus and motioned for Mr. Haddock to follow. Mr. Haddock made the conventional excuse to his wife and daughter and joined him.

"Now here's the point," began the man. "I'm in a jam."

"Oh!" said Mr. Haddock, relieved. "I thought you wanted to tell me a dirty story."

"No," said the man. "It's like this," and he mopped his brow nervously. "You see," he said, "to tell you the truth, I am a little worried about this sight-seeing trip."

"Why?" asked Mr. Haddock. "Has anything happened to the sights?"

"N-no," replied the man, "not exactly. But I'm a little afraid that I won't make good with the company."

"Nonsense!" said Mr. Haddock, giving him a hearty pat on the shoulder. "A man is as good as he looks."

"I know it," replied the guide. "But, you see," he confessed, twisting his fingers wretchedly with his hands, "the trouble is—I just got to Paris last night, and I've never been here before."

"Just the man for a guide," said Mr. Haddock.

The other flushed.

"Well," he said, "I was a guide in San Francisco once and I *look* like a guide."

"Yes," said Mr. Haddock, "you certainly do *look* like a guide."

"But I'm afraid ——" began the guide.

"Stop right there," said Mr. Haddock, and he put his hand impressively on the other's shoulder.

"Young man," he said, "nobody ever got anywhere by being afraid. In the bright lexicon of success there is no such word as 'can't.' If you *think* you can do a thing, you can *do* it. Look at Rockefeller."

The young man slowly straightened up and shook Mr. Haddock's hand.

"Thank you, sir," he said, simply. "I know I'm going to win."

"I know you are, too," said Mr. Haddock, "because you've got confidence in *yourself* now. Why, when I was a young man ——"

"Yes, sir," said the other, and he began walking rapidly toward the office.

"Aren't you going to let me tell you about when I was a young man?" called Mr. Haddock.

But the guide had already entered the building. Mr. Haddock shook his head and turned to the bus.

"Would anybody like to hear about when I was a young man?" he asked, but nobody seemed to pay any particular attention, so Mr. Haddock climbed up and asked the driver.

"Yes," replied he; and then he lowered his voice to a whisper, "but I'd rather have you tell me what is the name of this street we're on."

Mr. Haddock looked at him for a minute.

"This is going to be an interesting ride," he remarked.

"Well, you see, sir," explained the driver, "I just got the job this morning and I don't know Paris very well, but I don't want this fellow that's acting as guide to find out, because then I would lose my job."

Mr. Haddock put his hand on the man's shoulder. "What you need, young man," he said, "is confidence. Confidence in yourself."

"Yes, sir," replied the other.

"If you *believe* you can do anything, you can *do* it. The men who *succeed* are the men who don't know the *meaning* of the word, *'can't.'* In the bright lexicon of *success* ——" Mr. Haddock's voice was getting louder and louder as his enthusiasm increased.

The young man shook Mr. Haddock's hand. "Thank you, sir," he said. "I know I'm going to *win*."

"Good!" shouted Mr. Haddock.

The guide reappeared without his raincoat and climbed aboard; after a few minutes spent in fumbling with the various gears, the driver found the right one and the ride started. Just then it began to rain.

"Ladies and gentlemen," announced the guide, turning up his coat collar, "the first place to be visited by us on this memorable tour will be—will be ——" and he looked at Mr.

Haddock and then at the driver. Neither man returned the look.

"Will be," continued the guide, confidently, " 'Krumrine's tomb.' "

The driver looked up with a slight note of alarm and slowed down the car just a little.

"Krumrine's tomb," continued the guide, "was brought to Paris in 1853 as a gift of the school children."

Mr. Haddock turned to Mrs. Haddock. "Very interesting," he remarked.

"Very," said little Mildred.

The driver at that moment was passing a marble railing built around a staircase leading under the street, at one end of which was a sign marked "Metro."

"Krumrine's tomb," announced the guide, with a significant wave of his hand.

One of the ladies in the bus leaned out and very carefully took a photograph.

"Next," announced the guide, "we shall have unfolded before our eyes ——" and he once more looked appealingly at Mr. Haddock.

"Confidence," whispered Mr. Haddock, "that's all you need."

"We have," continued the guide, shouting very loudly, "the historic spot where took place that never-to-be-forgotten meeting between those two great generals and statesmen—Wellington," and he waved his hand to indicate where Wellington had stood, "and Robert E. Lee."

This was greeted by a real rebel yell and a considerable amount of applause from three Southern ladies on the last seat, and the guide bowed.

"May I ask a question?" said little Mildred.

"No," replied her father and the guide in one voice.

The bus swung around a corner, narrowly missing a *gendarme*.

"It's warm, isn't it?" said the guide.

"It sure is," replied the driver, and both wiped their foreheads vigorously.

"What's that building over there?" called a lady from the third seat.

"That one?" asked the guide.

"No," she said, pointing, "that one."

"Oh," said the guide, "*that* building," and he paused for a minute to take a breath.

"That building," he announced, "is one of the famous Defense d'Afficher buildings, erected for the national defense."

"Thank you," said the lady, and she made a note on a piece of paper.

By this time the driver had turned another corner.

"We are now approaching," announced the guide, "the Madeleine."

"My God!" whispered little Mildred, "he's right."

By this time it had stopped raining. The various people in the car who had raised their umbrellas now lowered them and the bus swung around in front of the Madeleine and turned to the right, up a narrow street.

"This street," said the guide, "was the favorite haunt of President Wilson when he was in Paris during the Peace Conference. And in that house over there," he announced, pointing, "was born the present President of France.

In fact," he added, "this is often called the Street of the Two Presidents.

"The driver will next take us," he shouted, "to that most famous of all French monuments, that Mecca of sight-seers and tourists from all over the world, that pearl of architecture —— I refer," said the guide, "to that sterling masterpiece of architectural brilliance, the Cathedral of St. Marks."

The driver groaned, but his groans were drowned in a torrent of applause.

Mr. Haddock got to his feet. "I move," he said, "that it be made unanimous."

This was followed by more applause, and before long, after winding its way through another narrow street, the auto bus turned once more to the right and they were back at the marble stairway marked "Metro."

The guide shot a quick glance at the driver and then jumped to his feet.

"Another and more intimate view," he announced, "of Krumrine's tomb," and the lady in the rear leaned out and took another photograph.

"And that building over there?"

"The Louvre," replied the guide; and then noticing some slight expression of doubt on her face, he quickly said, "The original Louvre."

"Oh!" said the lady. "Thank you." And she made some more notes on a piece of paper.

"And now we come," said the guide, glancing over his shoulder, "to that famous church ——"

"The Madeleine," chorused the first four rows of the bus.

"Right," said the guide, pleased.

Mrs. Haddock began to be a little restless.

"Will," she said, "I don't think those young men know what they're doing."

"Nonsense, dear!" said Mr. Haddock. "It's just because you and I are getting old. We mustn't become hidebound. We must let the younger generation take the wheel. And besides," he added, "it's sort of exciting. Let's take a chance and see where we go."

Mrs. Haddock shook her head.

"Oh, come on, mother," urged little Mildred. "Let's go around again."

But Mrs. Haddock remained firm, and so the bus was stopped and the Haddocks climbed down.

"You're doing fine," said Mr. Haddock, heartily, to the driver and the guide.

"Do you really think so, sir?" asked the guide. "There seems to be a little uneasiness among some of the passengers."

"Don't let that bother you at all," said Mr. Haddock. "That's to be expected when you're just starting out. It's mostly jealousy, anyway," he added.

So he shook hands, the guide climbed back into the car, Mr. Haddock waved a cheery *bon voyage* to the other passengers, and the bus started. And the last that the Haddocks saw of it the young guide was standing up in the front, pointing very confidently with one hand and yelling with the other very loudly through his megaphone.

"Well," said Mr. Haddock, "that took care

of an hour and a half all right and we've certainly seen the Madeleine."

"And Krumrine's tomb," added little Mildred.

Mrs. Haddock was looking very disappointedly through her guidebook.

"Will," she said, "you're not going to see *anything* of Paris."

"Why, Hattie," he remonstrated, "I've already seen an awful lot. I'm sorry, though, about Mildred."

"Don't mind about me," said the little girl. "I've seen a lot, too, and I don't hand what I've seen very much, anyway."

"I tell you," said Mr. Haddock, "what we'll do. Let's just pick three places—three places you didn't see yesterday."

"Well, all right," said Mrs. Haddock.

So they chose, first of all, the Sainte-Chapelle.

"That's the place, remember," said Mr. Haddock, "that the New York lady on the train told us to be sure and see."

The sun had come out and it was bright

afternoon when the Haddocks crossed over to the island in the Seine on which they were told they could find the Sainte-Chapelle.

It was the same island on which was located Notre-Dame, but the taxi pulled up in the middle of a number of official-looking buildings and they got out and went through a gate into a courtyard.

"It isn't very big," said Mrs. Haddock, disappointedly surveying the exterior of the chapel.

They entered a door and began climbing a very narrow, very winding staircase, down which was coming, greatly to their discomfort, a French family consisting of a father, a rather stout mother, and three children.

"It seems funny," puffed Mr. Haddock, as the visitors had squeezed past, "to think of French people sight-seeing."

"Yes," said Mildred, "and it makes me awful sore to hear those little kids speak French so well."

They resumed their climb.

"Gosh!" said Mr. Haddock, "this has got to be awful good to be worth all this effort."

And then suddenly they reached the top of the stairs and they were in the Sainte-Chapelle.

It was the first time, except for some churches at home, that Mr. Haddock had seen real colored glass, and it was the first time that Mr. Haddock realized the overwhelming effect of sunlight shining through windows a hundred times more beautiful than those at home. The walls, to Mr. Haddock, slowly became walls of flaming red and blue precious stones, and he closed his eyes.

The next stop was the Cluny Museum, across the river and over onto the left bank, and after wandering through large halls full of swords and armor, Mr. Haddock at last found himself alone in a small room. And as he stood there for a minute, the guide came up to him and in a rather mysterious whisper said, "It's over there," and pointed.

"*What's* over there?" asked Mr. Haddock, also in a low tone.

in Paris, France

But just at that moment Mrs. Haddock appeared.

"We'd better hurry," she said, "there's still eight or nine more rooms to walk through."

"Where's Mildred?" asked Mr. Haddock.

"She left me," replied Mrs. Haddock, "and said she wanted to look for something. We'll probably run into her."

So Mr. and Mrs. Haddock walked through eight or nine more rooms of various sizes filled with old pewter drinking cups, painted altar pieces, wood carvings, and ivories. And in the last room before going out they found Mildred walking rather frantically around and peering eagerly into all the cases.

"Come on, Mildred," said Mr. Haddock; "we've got to hurry."

"I won't hurry," said the little girl, "because I know it's here somewhere. Bobby Perkins saw it and I know it's *here*."

"*What's* here?" asked Mr. Haddock.

"The Ceinture de Chasteté," replied the little girl.

[263]

"What's she talking about, Will?" asked Mrs. Haddock.

"I don't know," replied Mr. Haddock, looking at his watch, "but if we're going to see any more of Paris this afternoon, we'll have to get a move on."

So little Mildred was carried, kicking and screaming, from the Cluny Museum and safely deposited in a taxicab.

"Now where?" asked Mr. Haddock.

"Let's stop and decide," said his wife.

So the taxicab pulled up beside the curb of a rather busy street while the three deliberated.

"It will either be," said Mrs. Haddock, "the Luxembourg Gardens or Napoleon's tomb, and possibly we'll have time for both."

Mr. Haddock was gazing across the street.

"Say," he said, slowly, "do you see what I see?"

Mildred looked. Mr. Haddock was pointing at a moving-picture theater.

"Charlot," read Mildred.

"Charlot nothing," said Mr. Haddock,

"look at the picture below. It's Charlie Chaplin."

He and his daughter exchanged significant glances.

"Or," said Mrs. Haddock, "we might possibly have time to get through a large part of the Louvre."

Mr. Haddock said nothing for a few minutes.

"Come, Will," said Mrs. Haddock. "Which will it be?"

"Look, dear," said Mr. Haddock, patting his wife on the knee. "You're tired, aren't you? You had a hard day yesterday and a hard day to-day and there will be all the packing to do to-morrow morning. Now Mildred and I," he went on, "would dearly love to see the Luxembourg Gardens and Napoleon's tomb and the Louvre. But we think," he concluded, "that it isn't fair to you to drag you to those places again."

"But, Will——" protested Mrs. Haddock.

"No, dear," said her husband, firmly, "Mil-

[265]

dred and I would rather sacrifice our own personal desires for your own good."

Mrs. Haddock's eyes narrowed as she looked at her husband.

"What's up?" she said. "What do you two want to do now?"

"We want to do whatever *you* want to do, dear," said Mr. Haddock, "but we just thought that maybe you were a little tired of sight-seeing and that maybe you would like to take a little rest—perhaps at a nice, comfortable movie."

"Well, of all things, Will Haddock!" Mrs. Haddock then stopped and considered. "Well——" she said at last.

"Good!" said Mr. Haddock.

So all three climbed out of the cab and went across the street and into the movie.

When they came out, it was close to six o'clock.

"Gosh!" said Mr. Haddock, as they were getting into a taxicab, "it seemed funny to see Charlie over here."

"I never liked him much," said Mrs. Haddock, "but it made me sort of homesick just the same."

When they were back at the hotel, there arose for the last time in Paris the problem of where to dine.

"The only thing we haven't done on Mrs. Jenkins's list," said Mrs. Haddock, consulting her notebook, "is to take dinner on the top of Montmartre. She says be *sure* and do it."

"All right," said Mr. Haddock, "but what will we do afterward?"

"Well," said Mrs. Haddock, "we really ought to go to the Opéra."

"That means dressing up, doesn't it?" said Mr. Haddock. "What's at the Opéra this week?"

Mrs. Haddock consulted the French newspaper that had come wrapped around Mr. Haddock's laundry.

"What is to-night?" she asked.

"Friday," replied Mr. Haddock.

"Vendredi," said Mildred.

Mrs. Haddock ran her finger down the newspaper. *"Vendredi,"* she announced, "Relâche."

Mr. Haddock considered thoughtfully. "Who's singing in it?"

Mrs. Haddock shook her head.

"I tell you what," said Mr. Haddock. "Of course, if you want to see the opera I'll be only too glad to go, but it seems to me that it might be better, for our last night, to enjoy something lighter."

"As, for instance," said little Mildred, "the Folies Bergères."

"Yes," said Mr. Haddock.

"What's the Folies Bergères?" asked Mrs. Haddock. "A play?"

"Well, no," said Mr. Haddock, "not exactly. As I understand it, it's sort of—sort of a musical comedy."

"With chorus girls?" asked Mrs. Haddock.

"Well," said Mr. Haddock, "possibly."

Mrs. Haddock took a long time to make up her mind.

"All right," she said at last, "but everybody will think it mighty funny that we didn't go to the opera. They'll think we didn't have a dress suit."

"We'll have our pictures taken in a dress suit," said Mr. Haddock, "and that will prove it."

The ride to the top of Montmartre proved longer and bumpier than the Haddocks had expected.

As they drove up the wide avenue toward the Opéra Mrs. Haddock's conscience stirred slightly.

"Will," she said, "this may be our last chance to see opera in Paris."

"Nonsense!" said Mr. Haddock. "We'll be coming back."

"When?" asked Mrs. Haddock.

Mr. Haddock was silent.

"Some day," he said at last.

By this time the cab was honking its way up a narrow street, and after a few turns there suddenly appeared in the distance above them a very high, very shiny white church with a dome that looked a little like a beehive and a little like the nipple of a baby's bottle.

"That's Sacré-Cœur," announced Mildred. "It cost over eight million dollars."

"That's a lot of money," said Mr. Haddock. "How much did Notre-Dame cost?"

"Not as much," replied little Mildred, "and it's bigger, too."

The taxicab stopped and the driver explained to Mildred that that was as far as he went.

"He says," she announced, "that we've got to take the *funiculaire* the rest of the way."

"Does *funiculaire* mean 'elevator'?" said Mr. Haddock, "because if it does ——" and he took out his watch and looked at it.

"No," said little Mildred, "it's a kind of a railway up the side of the hill."

So Mr. and Mrs. Haddock and Mildred bought tickets and got into the little car and soon they were slowly climbing toward Sacré-Cœuer.

"Oh dear!" said Mrs. Haddock, timidly looking back of her. "What if that cable should break?"

"Ha-ha-ha!" laughed Mr. Haddock, nervously wiping the perspiration from the palms of his hands. "Such a thing would be impossible in *this* day and generation."

At the middle of the incline, they passed the other car, which was going down. And in a few minutes, they were at the top.

"Let's eat first," said little Mildred.

So they began looking for what Mrs. Jenkins had recommended in her notebook as the "Place du Tertre."

Several tables were spread out in the open, and as there didn't seem to be any really first-class restaurants, the Haddocks finally sat down and ordered their dinner. And it was a fairly good dinner, too (although Mrs. Haddock did not exactly like the idea of eating in the street) and it was enlivened from time to time by old women who sang songs, old men who recited poetry, contortionists who turned somersaults, and a bearded gentleman who played the flute.

Then, when they had finished, they walked around in front of Sacré-Cœur and stood there for several minutes looking out over Paris. Finally Mrs. Haddock spoke.

"Will," she said, "I forgot to tell you that two of your shirts came back from the laundry all starched."

So they descended once more to the *funiculaire*.

When they at last reached the bottom there was no taxicab in sight and they began walking slowly down a narrow street until they came to a wide boulevard at what Mr. Haddock discovered was the Place Pigalle.

The Place seemed to be devoted entirely to cafés and restaurants whose brilliant electric signs invited one in strange red and blue lights to *"Soupers"* and *"Dancing."* Extending in both directions along the center of the boulevard was a street fair of some sort, with tents and monkeys and cowboys and a great many dizzy merry-go-rounds and steam swings.

"The French idea of pleasure," remarked Mr. Haddock philosophically, as they turned to the right and walked along the boulevard, "seems to be to see how much you can stand without getting sick."

All of the merry-go-rounds had pipe organs and all were playing at once; music of a more classical sort was coming from the orchestras in the different cafés; and that, combined with the cries of the various young girls who were being tossed about in the "American swings" and the looks which Mr. Haddock got from the highly painted young ladies who were walking aimlessly by, made the place seem very gay and very exciting.

They passed several curious places marked "Cabaret" with different names which Mr. Haddock did not understand, a great many more cafés, and then, just before they reached a large red electric sign of a windmill, they came to the Place Blanche and found a taxicab.

"There's the Moulin Rouge," said Mr. Haddock, pointing.

"Let's go in," said little Mildred.

"No," said Mrs. Haddock. "I tell you, Will, I don't like the atmosphere of this place."

[273]

"All right," said Mr. Haddock, "we'll go to the Folies Bergères."

But when they arrived at the Folies Bergères, Mrs. Haddock was not so sure that *that* was the place for Mr. Haddock, or little Mildred, *either,* and after the third tableau, which was called on the program: "Raymond et Whitcombe à Sodome et Gomorrhe," Mrs. Haddock rose firmly and decisively from her seat, took little Mildred by the hand, and started for the exit. Mr. Haddock followed, with occasional glances over his shoulder at the stage.

And they drove in silence to the hotel.

But when they were once more in their room and Mrs. Haddock and little Mildred were beginning to undress, Mr. Haddock revolted.

"Doggone it, Hattie!" he said, "this is our last night in Paris!"

"I've seen quite enough of Paris," said Mrs. Haddock.

"Won't you even just go somewhere and sit," asked her husband, "and watch people go by?"

"No," replied Mrs. Haddock. "I don't want to watch these kind of people go by."

"*This* kind of people," corrected little Mildred. "Can I go with you, father?"

"Sure," said Mr. Haddock.

"Mildred," said Mrs. Haddock, "is going to stay right here and go to bed. We've got a hard day to-morrow. And if you want to go, Will Haddock," she added, "that's up to you."

Mr. Haddock hesitated.

"Well," he said at last, "I'll go for a little while."

So he went downstairs and out the door, and in a minute or two he had found a taxi.

"Just drive around a bit," he said, after deliberating a minute.

The driver replied with a long sentence in French, evidently a question.

"I said, 'Just drive *around* a bit,' " repeated Mr. Haddock, and he tried to express with gestures what he meant, but with no better result.

"Oh, all right!" he said, giving up the fight. "To the Folies Bergères."

But when Mr. Haddock had sat through a good bit of the rest of the Folies Bergères, he began frankly to be a little bored. As a matter of fact, he had seen much better shows in New York; the only acts that appealed to him and the rest of the audience seemed to be American acts; and there was a man in the rear of the house who annoyed Mr. Haddock very much by clapping very loudly and very artificially at the end of each number. So, all in all, in spite of the momentary excitement of having strange young ladies make strange old proposals to him in the lobby of the theater, Mr. Haddock was quite glad when the show was over. But he still didn't want to go to bed.

He wandered slowly down a well-lighted street called the Rue Montmartre, or something like that, past the Palace Theatre where the Dolly Sisters were playing in something called "Oh Absolument Shocking," until he came to the large boulevard on which he knew was situated the Café de la Paix. But as he was walking along in that direction, a man suddenly stepped up to him and said, "Do you want a guide?"

"No thank you," said Mr. Haddock. "I did all my sight-seeing this afternoon."

"I don't mean that," said the man, with a shifty glance around. "How would you like to see ——" and he named one or two things.

And then Mr. Haddock got suddenly and unexpectedly very angry. It was something that had been growing in him ever since the fourth or fifth tableau at the Folies Bergères, and he felt now, all of a sudden, the unusual but very strong desire to give this disgusting panderer a good sock in the eye. And the "guide" must have sensed that feeling in Mr. Haddock, too, for he immediately turned and walked rapidly away, and after his disappearance Mr. Haddock found himself trembling so violently that he had to go to the nearest café and have two glasses of beer before he once more felt like venturing farther along that street.

And then, at peace once more, it occurred to him that it might be nice to drive down and see

[277]

Notre-Dame in the moonlight for the last time before he went to bed. So he paid for the two saucers which represented the two beers, refused for the eighth time to buy a rug from the sidewalk Armenian salesman, and walked over to a taxi.

"Do you speak English?" he asked the driver.

"*Oui,* monsieur," was the eager reply.

"Well," said Mr. Haddock, "this is my last night in Paris and I'd like to drive through the Tuileries Gardens, then to the Seine, and then slowly down along the river until we get to Notre Dame. Do you understand?"

"*Oui,* monsieur," replied the driver.

So they started.

But after a little while Mr. Haddock noticed that they were climbing and it occurred to him that possibly they were climbing once more in the direction of Montmartre. But Mr. Haddock was quite humble as to his knowledge of Paris compared with that of a taxi driver and he sat back, with more or less confidence, to wait for the Tuileries Gardens. In a few minutes the taxicab dashed up a narrow street and stopped outside a place over which was an electric sign *"Au Zelli's."* An extremely polite uniformed attendant opened Mr. Haddock's taxicab door and waited.

"Is this the way to Notre-Dame?" asked Mr. Haddock, pleasantly.

The man smiled and said something in French to the driver who suddenly turned and overwhelmed Mr. Haddock and the doorman with a torrent of abuse.

"He says," translated the doorman, "that you told him to come here."

"But I didn't," remonstrated Mr. Haddock.

This was followed by another even more lively conversation between the two Frenchmen. Mr. Haddock sat back and waited.

Three large bus-loads of young American men suddenly drew up along the curb in front of him. Each man was carrying in his hand a small Yale flag. They climbed down from the bus, formed in a column, and marched in the door of Zelli's.

Mr. Haddock, his curiosity aroused, settled

the argument with the taxi driver by paying double the amount shown on the taxi meter, got out, and followed the young men. Just as he was going in, three more huge sight-seeing busses arrived. These were decorated with Harvard flags.

"It looks like it's going to be a good game," he remarked to the doorman.

When he finally got inside there was a good deal of confusion, but suddenly Mr. Haddock felt his hand being shaken in a very enthusiastic greeting. A smiling individual whom everybody had been calling "Joe" and who looked a little like an Italian was welcoming him and asking him if he wanted the "Royal Box."

Mr. Haddock smiled, but shook his head.

"I'll just watch," he said, "from the side lines."

In a few minutes the whistle blew and the game was on. In the first period, Yale seemed to have a slight advantage, due to their superior numbers and the fact that one member of the team had been to bed the night before.

But in the second quarter, Harvard discovered the weak spot in the Yale defense and by pouring champagne into him on every other play they soon had the whole left side of the Yale line groggy and a little bewildered.

The score at the end of the first half stood: "Harvard, 200 francs—Yale, 900 francs." Cheers and songs and coat checks were enthusiastically exchanged.

In between the halves the interest was heightened by the unexpected arrival of two bus-loads full of energetic Good Will girls who had been sent over to France by Anne Morgan, or somebody, to view the battlefields and thereby to increase the good will between France and America in case of another war.

Mr. Haddock, in the meantime, had found the bar, which really wasn't very hard to find, and in a manner which he never could quite understand he discovered that he was enthusiastically buying champagne for three or four very nice-looking French girls whom he could not remember ever having seen before. It was all very jolly and very pleasant, and the two white-coated men behind the bar were working very fast and Mrs. Zelli was sitting at the other end of the bar behind the cash register, so Mr. Haddock decided not to go back to see the second half of the game.

Occasional cheers came to him from time to time, but he soon gradually lost all interest in everything except these quite remarkable girls who were named, respectively, Paulette, Renée, and Sarah.

"Will you dance wiz me?" finally asked one of the girls for whom Mr. Haddock had just bought a package of rose-tipped Abdulah cigarettes.

"Sure," said Mr. Haddock, "why not?" So they squeezed their way along the outside of the bar through a lot of young girls and men on to the dance floor.

The game had evidently ended and the various participants were being carried to their corners or out to taxicabs, and Mr. Haddock, who had had some doubts as to his dancing ability, inasmuch as he had not been on a dance floor for seventeen years, suddenly discovered that he was not so bad at the Tango, after all, and as his confidence returned and the music grew wilder Mr. Haddock began making up steps of his own—steps he had always wanted to do, but had never quite had the opportunity.

He was just really getting started, however, when the music stopped, but he applauded loudly and vigorously and finally conceived the idea of giving the orchestra leader the sum of five hundred francs, which was accepted, and the music began again. This time Mr. Haddock found that he could really do better without Paulette because there were a lot of the steps that she didn't quite follow and then, after a little while, he found that he wasn't bumping into quite so many people and toward the end of the dance Mr. Haddock, greatly to his joy, had the floor all to himself.

The orchestra ended with a crash and Mr. Haddock, after three or four minutes, stopped dancing and a scene of the wildest enthusiasm ensued. Ladies ran up and kissed him, men in evening clothes shook him by the hand, cheers sounded from all over the room, and Mr. Haddock, flushed and happy, was escorted back to the bar.

"I want to call up my wife," he announced, happily. "She ought to be here." And he started for a telephone.

But Mr. Haddock never reached the telephone and that was all he remembered, and when he opened his eyes he was lying in bed at the hotel and Mrs. Haddock was standing looking at him.

"Hello, dear!" he said, trying to smile. "Did I wake you up?"

Mrs. Haddock said nothing.

Mr. Haddock attempted to rise. "Well," he said cheerfully, "you should have come with me. It was a lot of fun." And then he noticed that he was wearing only the top of his pajamas and that in his hand was the remnants of a bunch of roses.

"I brought you some flowers," he announced, with another smile, "but they must have got mussed."

"You needn't explain," said Mrs. Haddock

[284]

grimly. "The gentleman who brought you home told me all about it."

"What gentleman?" said Mr. Haddock, defiantly. "I came home alone."

"That's all right," said Mrs. Haddock. "You get up now and take a bath, and hurry, because the train goes at one thirty. . . . Mildred," she called, "are you all packed?"

Mildred came into the room, looked at her father, and began to laugh.

"So this is Paris!" she said.

And at one thirty (or thirteen thirty, as the time-table said) the Haddocks and their baggage were in their compartment in the train, and as the car slowly began to move forward Mrs. Haddock reached up in her suitcase and took down a guidebook, little Mildred went out to look for a drink of water, and Mr. Haddock closed his eyes for a short nap.

New Harper Novels

THE APPLE OF THE EYE   By GLENWAY WESCOTT

Of Glenway Wescott's remarkable novel Sinclair Lewis writes: "Fine and fiery art. . . . I am afraid he has something curiously like genius." The scene of this spiritual tragedy is a little known countryside of southern Wisconsin. Because of an ever-present sense of the pathetic and the terrible and an extraordinary ability to create character, Glenway Wescott has written a memorable story, one that is sure to be read with emotion and talked about with enthusiasm.

A PRINCE OF MALAYA   By SIR HUGH CLIFFORD

To those who read Sir Hugh Clifford's "Malayan Monochromes" this volume needs no recommendation; to those who have not it will be sufficient to say that Conrad was his friend and admirer. This novel is a brilliant study of the Oriental temperament by a writer who knows the East as well as Conrad or Kipling.

DESERT: A LEGEND   By MARTIN ARMSTRONG

The action of this story moves between the corrupt brilliance of pagan Alexandria and desert where Christian ascetics sought salvation. A subtle and moving drama of abnegation, it is told with simplicity and beauty, with understanding of the religious temperament, and with dramatic power.

THE SACRED GIRAFFE   By S. MADARIAGA

"As witty a bit of fooling as we have read since the ironies of Samuel Butler, and not unworthy to be mentioned as in the apostolic succession from 'Erewhon,'" wrote the *London Daily Telegraph* of this brilliant and spirited satire. This fantastic tale merrily satirizes the follies of the present day in a civilized and ingenious manner.

HARPER & BROTHERS

Publishers Since 1817   NEW YORK

Unusual Memoirs

MY LIFE AND TIMES   By JEROME K. JEROME.

The life story of Jerome K. Jerome, famous author of "Three Men in a Boat" and "The Passing of the Third Floor Back," who during his varied career has been clerk, teacher, journalist, actor, editor and novelist, and has known most of the outstanding men and women of his time. His book is packed with delightful observations and anecdotes, and gives an inimitable cross-section of the literary and theatrical England of the past half century.

MORE UNCENSORED RECOLLECTIONS   ANONYMOUS

The English author of "Uncensored Recollections," that daring volume which excited so much discussion recently, again lifts the curtain which hangs between the private life of the great and the public. With pungent humor and the utmost frankness, the author, who belongs obviously to the society of which he writes, tells of court and official life in England and the European capitals.

A MUSICIAN AND HIS WIFE   By MRS. REGINALD DE KOVEN

The crowded memoirs of a crowded career—of one who as wife of a famous composer led a life of unsurpassed interest and was intimate with all the great personalities of the eighteen seventies, eighties, and nineties.

SOME MEN AND WOMEN OF IMPORTANCE By A. G. GARDINER

As editor for nearly twenty years of the London *Daily News*, A. G. Gardiner has had unique opportunities for intimate contacts with leaders of opinion and action all over the world. In this book he presents a strikingly varied gallery of stimulating word-portraits—of Stanley Baldwin, Lady Astor, Ramsay MacDonald, Bernard Shaw, Charlie Chaplin, W. J. Bryan, Calvin Coolidge and many others.

THROUGH MANY WINDOWS   By HELEN WOODWARD

One of the most interesting of modern business women writes of her extraordinary career in advertising and other fields; combining with her autobiography much shrewd and dispassionate comment on modern business life.

HARPER & BROTHERS

Publishers Since 1817   NEW YORK

bw. St 495 mp